"I don't think dancing is such a good idea."

Even as she spoke, Dena's body moved in time with Gabe's, as if by instinct.

She glanced around nervously as their former classmates gathered on the sidelines to gawk. Gil Reyes called out. "Objection—counsel is leading the witness!"

"Don't you think we've given this crowd enough to talk about?" she murmured.

"No," Gabe said. "Not yet."

He ambushed her with a kiss—the swift, ruthless, take-no-prisoners variety. From their former classmates came shouts and whistles of encouragement.

Gabe cranked it up a notch, pouring everything he had into the kiss. Their audience responded with hooting, foot-stomping applause.

This was kissing as a spectator sport. This kiss made a statement: loud, clear, unambiguous.

Gabe wanted her so badly, it was a physical ache. At that moment he'd have done anything, sacrificed anything, to undo the mistakes of his past.

Dear Reader,

Harlequin Temptation celebrates its fifteenth birthday this year! When we launched in 1984, our goal was to be the most sensual, most contemporary series in the marketplace. Today we're still that—and *more*. Each month we bring you four fun sexy stories that range from romantic fantasy to "Blazing" sensuality. Temptation is *the* series for women of the new Millennium.

Over the years popular authors such as Jayne Ann Krentz, Barbara Delinsky, LaVyrle Spencer and Carla Neggers have contributed to the success of Temptation. Many of our writers have gone on to achieve fame and fortune—and the *New York Times* bestseller list!

In celebration of our fifteen years, I'm delighted to introduce you to three shining stars. Say hello to Pamela Burford, Alison Kent and Donna Sterling who are each thrilled to bring you their sizzling stories in September, October and November.

I hope you enjoy these talented authors, as I hope you will enjoy all the fabulous books and authors to come.

Happy Reading!

Birgit Davis-Todd
Senior Editor, Harlequin Books

P.S. We love to hear from readers! Write and tell us what your favorite Temptation book was over the past fifteen years. We'll publish a list of the top fifty!

Harlequin Books
225 Duncan Mill Road
Don Mills, Ontario
CANADA M3B 3K9

A CLASS ACT
Pamela Burford

9776

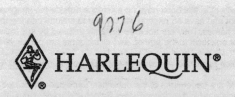

HARLEQUIN®

TORONTO • NEW YORK • LONDON
AMSTERDAM • PARIS • SYDNEY • HAMBURG
STOCKHOLM • ATHENS • TOKYO • MILAN • MADRID
PRAGUE • WARSAW • BUDAPEST • AUCKLAND

To my sister Kate Burford,
with gratitude for her constant enthusiasm
and for cheerfully sharing her vast store of knowledge,
several tidbits of which have found their way
into this book.

ISBN 0-373-25846-1

A CLASS ACT

Copyright © 1999 by Pamela Burford Loeser.

Printed in U.S.A.

Dear Reader,

I was thrilled and honored when Harlequin asked me to write one of the three books celebrating Temptation's fifteenth anniversary. To me, this line represents everything special about romance: the excitement, the sensuality, the wonder of new love.

My Harlequin novels have made me a two-time finalist in both Romance Writers of America's RITA Awards and *Romantic Times*'s Reviewers Choice Awards. I'm very excited to be working on a four-book Temptation miniseries to be published next year.

I'd love to know what you thought of *A Class Act*. Send a SASE to: Pamela Burford, P.O. Box 1321, North Baldwin, NY 11510-0721. I'll mail you an autographed bookplate, and imprinted emery board and an excerpt from my next book. If you surf the Web, check out my home page at www.pamelaburford.com. You'll find book excerpts, a contest, and a section called Temptation in the Kitchen, featuring recipes for Ham Conklin's Smoked Brisket with Bourbon Mop and some of the other dishes my characters like to cook!

Keep reading!

Pamela Burford

1

SHE'S NOT COMING.

Gabe Moreau scanned the packed ballroom for the hundredth time since he'd arrived ten minutes ago, while attempting to feign interest in Rhonda Peterson's incessant blathering.

Rhonda nodded toward a tall, balding man Gabe didn't recognize, and whom he probably hadn't spoken two words to back in high school. "And Howard Tibbs has his own plumbing supply store here in Briarfield. Well, it was his father's business, but his dad retired to Boca. Speaking of going into Daddy's business—did I hear you were made a partner?"

Rhonda grinned, displaying a mouthful of big capped teeth lined up like marble tombstones. Gabe carefully avoided staring at the speck of spinach lodged between her incisors.

He nodded. "That's right."

"And Andrea, too." Her eyes glittered with curiosity as she glanced across the room at the lady in question, now sharing a laugh with Mike Ames, if Gabe wasn't mistaken. He'd heard Mike had done well for himself in commercial real estate. Obviously Andrea had heard the same thing.

That was all Gabe needed—Rhonda the class busybody spreading more rumors about himself and Andrea Pittman. Despite the passage of fifteen years, he suspected Rhonda Peterson was the same compulsive gossipmonger she'd been back in high school.

He watched Andrea for a moment, doing what she always did at social functions, diligently working the room, now ferreting out former classmates who'd done well for themselves and might be in the market for legal services. The woman had a bloodhound's nose for money, and the bullheaded determination required to steer that money into the firm. Every day, in every way, she made her daddy—and his—so very proud.

"We both made partner at the same time," he said.

"The two of you really lucked out, with both your dads being founding partners of such a prestigious law firm."

Gabe stopped scrutinizing the crowd and gave Rhonda his full attention. "I prefer to think luck didn't have much to do with it."

"Well…I just meant…I didn't mean to imply you didn't *deserve* to—"

"Of course not. I'm sure you realize that Moreau Pittman didn't get to be one of the top firms on Wall Street by practicing blind nepotism. Andrea is one hell of a lawyer." Hardworking, ruthless, and driven, she would have excelled in any firm. But like him, she'd chosen to direct her efforts toward the family business. It was what they'd both wanted since they were children.

That wasn't all Andrea had wanted, and observing the speculative gleam in Rhonda's eye, Gabe suspected he'd never live down his past.

Which was probably no more than he deserved. Suddenly he wished he hadn't come here tonight, to the Briarfield Country Club of all places, a venue he avoided whenever possible, along with the shameful memories that went with it.

There was only one reason he'd broken down and accepted the invitation to his fifteen-year high-school reunion, and she was a no-show. He'd deliberately arrived late, well into the cocktail hour that preceded dinner, in the hope that she'd already be there when he made his entrance. But apparently she'd had more sense than he, and had blown off the reunion.

A paunchy man with curly black hair, a trim beard and a barroom tan joined them. He slapped Gabe on the shoulder, and only quick footwork saved Gabe's snowy white tuxedo shirt from the dark Beaujolais that sloshed out of his wineglass.

"Gabe Moreau! I'd recognize you anywhere!" the man crowed, before lowering his voice. "This place must bring back some hot memories for you, huh?"

Rhonda bit her lip to stifle a smirk. Gabe glanced at the man's name badge. Frank Runkey, Jr. He couldn't believe it. This puffy, jowly loudmouth was the guy all the girls had mooned over? Clearly the years had not been kind to "Hunky" Runkey.

Gabe extended his hand and Frank pumped it. "How have you been, Frank?"

"Not as good as you. Hear you're a partner now. And not just you." His lascivious gaze flicked to Andrea. "How's your golf *score* lately? Huh?"

Gabe pretended not to hear the special emphasis. "I play tennis now."

Frank laughed. "Tennis! I've never done it on a

clay court myself. Might give it a try, if I could be on the bottom."

"Frank!" Rhonda giggled, elbowing him. "You're so bad."

"If you'll excuse me," Gabe muttered, turning his back on them. He deposited his wineglass on a table as he made his way toward the exit.

"Headed out to the fairways, Gabe?" Dave Messina snickered as he passed. "Nice night for a hole in one."

Gabe didn't acknowledge the comment, nor did he so much as blink when someone else added, "How's that driver of yours holding up?"

A high, whiny voice that could only be Bruce Lakeland all grown up put in, "Oh, I bet it's got a few good strokes left. Huh, Gabe? A few good strokes?"

He was nearly at the exit when someone called out, *"Fore!"* prompting a burst of laughter. He glanced at Andrea and saw those near her watching for her reaction, whispering behind their hands. A brick-red blush crawled upward from the low, square neckline of her elegant custom designer gown, a beaded sheath in seafoam-green silk that complemented her petite figure. She pinned Gabe with the flat, hard stare she'd perfected in the courtroom.

As if the smarmy innuendos were his fault! *Hate to break it to you, babe*, he wanted to tell her, *but you've got no one to blame but yourself.*

Distracted, he strode blindly through the open double doorway and barreled into someone just entering. Murmuring apologies, he caught the woman by her bare upper arms as her stiletto heels flew out from under her. He hauled her up, steadying her.

In the next instant he was struck dumb. His heart slammed into his ribs like a wrecking ball. Because he knew. Before she'd even straightened to her impressive height, before she'd tossed her chin-length silver-blond curls off her face, before she'd looked him in the eye. He knew.

"Well. I was hoping to make a memorable entrance," Dena Devlin said, with that distinctive lopsided smile he hadn't seen in fifteen years. "Thanks, Gabe."

She shook out her hair and casually straightened her flamboyant multicolored dress. It was tied at one shoulder and wrapped fluidly around her body, with enough tucks and folds to conform to a figure that was even more full and womanly than he remembered.

At the moment, Dena matched his six-foot-two-inch height, though he knew her to be five eleven in her stocking feet. There weren't many women her size with the confidence to wear three-inch heels, but then, the Dena Devlin he'd known had never been one to run with the herd.

Her knee-length dress, he now saw, appeared to be tissue-thin linen boldly printed with some Eastern-looking design in rainbow hues. The bow on one shoulder holding the whole thing on looked like it would spring open with her next deep breath. A dozen bangle bracelets in tortoiseshell and hammered silver jangled on her wrists. Matching earrings brushed her suntanned shoulders.

Before Gabe could gather his wits and formulate

some artfully offhand comment, Dena sailed past with a breezy "Where's the food? I'm famished!"

Just like that. As if they'd been nothing more than casual acquaintances all those years ago.

He turned and watched her set a direct course for the nearest hors d'oeuvre-toting waiter, greeting former classmates along the way. Her scent lingered in his nostrils, the unique essence of her skin and hair, overlaid with a subtle and exotically voluptuous perfume she'd probably concocted herself.

Those towering heels and that body-hugging outfit did incredible things to her fanny, which swayed provocatively with every step she took away from him. Gabe was reminded of Jack Lemmon's apt description of a luscious rear view of Marilyn Monroe in the movie *Some Like It Hot:* "Like Jell-O on springs."

She hadn't blown off the reunion after all.

AFTER THAT spectacular entrance, Dena studiously avoided looking at Gabe. She didn't need eyes to track his movements; her female radar had gone into overdrive the instant she'd recognized him. She sensed him off to the side now, sensed his eyes on her as he hobnobbed with some of their old pals.

Many times she'd imagined what he must look like in his thirties, but her imagination had fallen short. His face had matured—the angles sharper, the furrows deeper, the whiskey-colored eyes more intense. His thick light brown hair was neatly trimmed, combed off his face.

Gabe's once rangy basketball player's body had filled out. His shoulders were wider than she remembered, his chest deeper. Even his neck was thicker. After that initial body slam on her way in here, Dena knew it was all hard, unyielding muscle under that elegant black tux, which had obviously been custom-tailored to his frame. He'd easily supported her weight as she'd struggled to get her feet under her, and Lord knew she was no dainty little thing.

Dena perused her surroundings. So this was the Briarfield Country Club, the place she hadn't been good enough to set foot in fifteen years ago. She took in the high, carved ceiling with its ornamental coving and glittering chandeliers; the two massive wooden fireplaces, filled now in mid-July with flower arrangements that matched the centerpieces on the linen-draped tables; the open French doors leading to the flagstone piazza strung with tiny white lights, and the terraced gardens beyond; the elegant string quartet in one corner, providing a mellow musical backdrop for the hum of conversation, the muted tinkle of silver and china.

The sights, the sounds, the smell of money, most of it old.

This was where it had happened. Not here precisely, but somewhere out there on that manicured golf course.

The bastard.

As Dena heaped her little plate high with mini shrimp burritos and skewered chicken with Thai peanut sauce, Rhonda bustled up to welcome her and fill her in on Steve Brock's latest boyfriend and the history of Nancy Lord's breast implants. Dena supposed it was comforting to know some things never changed.

She said, "Rhonda, you've got a big piece of spinach stuck between your teeth."

"Oh!" Rhonda covered her mouth and half turned away, then flashed those mammoth choppers at Dena, who gave her a thumbs-up. As a teenager, Rhonda had worn her thick chestnut hair shoulder length. Now it was cut in a short, serviceable style that made her look downright matronly.

"You forgot to pick up your name badge on the way in," Rhonda said, waving the thing in Dena's face.

"I don't think anyone will have trouble recognizing me." Dena exchanged a wave with Mindy Shwartz over Rhonda's shoulder. "Unless I'm wearing a badge that says 'Geraldine Devlin.'" As this one did. No one had had the nerve to call her Geraldine since she'd bloodied Hunky Runkey's nose for doing so in the second grade.

"But everyone's wearing one. I did them up on my computer. See? I found clip art that looks just like our mascot, the Briarfield Bulldog."

Dena swallowed a mouthful of burrito. "Oh, is that a bulldog? I thought it was Mr. Carpenter," she said, referring to the man who was still Briarfield High's principal.

Rhonda laughed.

"No, really," Dena insisted. "Take a good look."

Rhonda squinted at the small image adorning one corner of the badge. Her face sagged.

"Oh, there's Ham!" Dena cried.

"Ham?" Rhonda looked up. "Oh, Mr. Conklin. Didn't he retire the year we graduated?"

"I'll talk to you later." Dena pushed through the crowd and hurled herself at Ham Conklin in a one-armed embrace, while trying to keep the contents of her plate from sliding to the floor. He returned her bear hug with a strength that belied his eighty years.

"Still going for the preppy look, I see," Ham said, grabbing hold of her free hand and looking her up and down.

"I have your restrained example to follow."

Ham Conklin had always been one of a kind. Dena noted a deepening network of lines in his face, but those smiling hazel eyes remained as sharp as ever. The top and sides of his longish silver hair were pulled back and secured in a short pony-tail, leaving the strands at his nape free. While all of the other men present wore tuxes or dark suits, Ham sported a colorful dashiki shirt over calf-length olive-green clamdigger pants. His long, bony feet were shoved into a pair of huaraches.

Dena didn't connect him to the woman standing nearby until he put his arm around her. "Reba Singer, Dena Devlin."

In looks, Reba Singer was the antithesis of Ham Conklin. Short and a bit zaftig, she wore a sequined royal-blue mother-of-the-bride dress, which matched her eyes and blue-tinted, stiffly coiffed hair. A blue satin clutch bag and dyed-to-match pumps completed the conservative ensemble. Dena guessed her to be no more than sixty, a full two decades younger than Ham. He must have hooked up with her since the last time Dena had seen him, about a year ago.

"I'm a former student," Dena said, reaching out to shake the other woman's hand.

Reba's grip was firm; her smile radiated a homey warmth. "I know. Ham has spoken of you."

"Don't believe a word of it," Dena joked, glad that her beloved favorite teacher had found someone special after four decades as a widower. "How long have you two been, uh..." She peeked at Reba's left ring finger and found it bare.

"Oh, we're not married," Reba said, "just living together."

"I've been trying to get her to tie the knot for months," Ham said, "but the shameless hussy prefers to live in sin."

Reba gave a nonchalant wave. "What's the rush?"

"You're still planning to stay at my place this week, right?" Ham asked Dena.

"That invitation better still be open. I don't have hotel reservations."

The reunion committee, spearheaded by Rhonda Peterson, had planned a full week of activities out here on Long Island's North Fork. Driving home to New Jersey every night would have been impractical, and Ham had generously offered Dena a room in his sprawling home, which he'd converted to a bed-and-breakfast inn when he retired from teaching.

Ham looked over Dena's shoulder. "Here's someone else I want you to meet, Reba."

Dena's internal radar sounded the alarm even before Gabe joined them. She kept her genial smile firmly in place as Ham introduced him to Reba.

"If it weren't for your significant other here," Gabe told Reba, "I doubt I'd have graduated with my sanity intact. Ham was more than an English teacher and drama coach. He was an adviser, a confidant, not to mention a much-needed buffer between me and the running-dog imperialists who he claimed ran the school."

"And still run it," Ham grumbled. "Speaking of running dogs, I'd like to congratulate whoever drew this picture of Old Man Carpenter and added the bulldog ears." He flicked his name badge. "That kind of satire should be applauded."

"That would be Rhonda Peterson," Dena said. "I'm sure she'll appreciate that you noticed."

Ham and Reba bade them adieu and went in search of Rhonda, leaving Dena and Gabe alone. Dena lifted a bamboo skewer from her plate and nibbled a chunk of grilled chicken. Gabe stood watching her, silently sipping his martini. No *How's life been treating you?* No *Gee, I've missed you.* No *Please forgive me, I was an idiot.* He just stood there waiting for her to say something.

Fine. If that was the way he wanted it.

Dena glanced around the sumptuously appointed room. "So. At last I get to see the inside of this place."

His fingers tightened on the stem of his glass, sending ripples through the clear liquid, and she knew her barb had found its target.

She added, "You must've been pleased they decided to hold this wingding here. Your old stomping grounds. So to speak."

She was goading him and enjoying it. He stared at her a few moments, then casually glanced around as if to ensure their conversation was private. "I suppose I should feel honored. You're actually talking to me."

"Did you expect me to ignore you?"

One broad shoulder lifted negligently. "Why not? You managed to do it for a whole two months before graduation."

A venomous reply sprang to her lips, and it was all she could do to tamp it down. The impulse shocked her. She'd managed to swallow her anguish all those years ago, when she was a timid, insecure adolescent from the wrong side of the tracks. She'd held it all in then, the pain, the humiliation.

And everyone had known. She'd wrapped her hurt up hard and tight inside, but everyone had known and she'd had to see that knowledge in their smirking faces every day for two months, hear it in their snickering whispers.

No. After what she'd endured back then, Dena wasn't about to make a fool of herself over Gabe Moreau at this late date.

She asked, "How are your parents?"

He plucked a half-eaten mini burrito off her plate and popped it in his mouth. The act irked her, with its implied intimacy. He had no right to imply any such thing. She handed the half-full plate to a passing waiter.

"They're the same as you remember," he said. "If anything, a little more set in their ways." He appeared bored by the subject.

"Tell them the janitor's daughter says hi."

His gaze snapped to her face. For an unguarded instant she saw the old Gabe, the Gabe she'd thought she'd known. "Dena——"

"You two getting reacquainted?" Dave Messina materialized at her side, along with a rotund man she didn't recognize until she glanced at his name badge. She tried not to gape. *Hunky Runkey?* It couldn't be!

She caught Gabe's eye and they shared a silent exchange. Just like old times. His lips twitched, and she bit the inside of her cheek struggling to keep a straight face. Then Frank opened his mouth and any doubts she'd had evaporated.

"Hey, Gabe, I thought you were headed out to the golf course," he said, swirling the ice in his highball glass. "Guess you changed your mind. I don't see any grass stains on that nice tux."

Gabe stiffened and glanced at Dena.

"Maybe he's looking for the right partner," Dave said, with a smarmy grin. "One who knows how to keep a tight grip on the shaft."

Gabe's eyes glittered dangerously. His gaze flicked from Dave and Frank to Dena, and she realized with a start that he was concerned for her sake. No doubt he recalled how easily intimidated she used to be, and didn't want her publicly embarrassed. The gallant impulse sent a little thrill through her—for about a nanosecond, until she remembered that it was long overdue. If he'd had her welfare in mind all those years ago, these two blowhards wouldn't have anything to joke about now.

Clearly Frank was just getting warmed up. When he opened his mouth to speak again, Gabe skewered him with a glacial look and growled, "I think we've heard en—"

"So you guys are into golf?" Dena asked, with wide-eyed innocence.

The three men stared at her, mute.

"Because I don't know much about the game myself, but I'm interested in learning," she said, staring down at Dave, half a head shorter than she. "Like for instance, I thought you were supposed to hold the club by the grip, not the shaft."

Dave stood blinking for a few moments and finally mumbled, "Uh, yeah, that's right."

She turned to Frank. "My friend Margaret plays a lot of golf, but I don't recall her ever coming back with any grass stains. Maybe she's not doing it right?"

Frank sent an imploring glance to the other men. Dave backed up a step. Gabe, wearing a silky little smile, took a lingering sip of his martini.

"Oh, I know!" she said, with guileless enthusiasm. "Maybe you get those grass stains when you kneel down to line up your putts."

Gabe's drink seemed to go down the wrong way. He sputtered, his eyes watering. A lifelong New Yorker, he didn't need to be told that *putz* was melting-pot vernacular for the male organ.

And neither did Frank, who flinched as she sidled closer to him. He was probably wondering whether she realized what she'd said, and dreading the next words out of her mouth.

She smoothed out a wrinkle in the collar of Frank's jacket, stretched to the bursting point over his rotund gut. "I adore men in evening dress. I don't think I've ever seen a tux in this color."

"I got to the rental place early for the best selection. Oh say, isn't that the Forsyth twins? I've gotta go say hi."

Dave quickly jumped in with, "Me, too."

"Well, don't stay away too long," Dena told their retreating backs. "I have more questions about golf."

She watched them hightail it across the room before turning back to Gabe, who raised his glass in a silent salute. The gesture sparked a giddy warmth in her chest, even as she chided herself for caring.

Someone behind Dena began clapping. She spun around and found herself face-to-face with a man she couldn't place, though the features were vaguely familiar. He was around her age but prematurely gray, with an athlete's build and smiling eyes as dark and mellow as molasses. Yum.

"Brava," he said. "Though I was kind of looking forward to watching Gabe lay into those two."

She glanced at the man's name badge, but his quick reflexes won out. He slapped his hand over it and gave her a challenging grin.

"No fair," Dena said. Who was this mystery man? And how could she have trouble remembering a guy this attractive and personable?

"Gabe knows," the man said. "Don't you?"

Dena turned to see Gabe regarding the newcomer with something akin to awe. "Scott Cafferty?"

As soon as he said it, Dena saw it, too. Her mouth dropped open. Scott uncovered his badge, and she checked it just to make sure. As startling as Hunky Runkey's transformation was, Scott had him beat. Last time she'd seen him, he'd been an awkward, pimply jock with squinty eyes, thick horn-rimmed glasses, and a black buzz cut. His skin had cleared, he'd switched to contacts, and the hair...

Gabe said, "I wouldn't have recognized you on the street. You've got kind of a Richard Gere thing going there."

Scott dragged his fingers through his thick salt-

and-pepper hair. "The way I figure it, Gere's got a Scott Cafferty thing going."

Dena sobered. "I heard about Annie. I'm really sorry."

Gabe echoed the sentiment. Scott had married his high-school sweetheart, Annie Goode, shortly after graduation. Less than two years later she'd died of a brain tumor, after a tough battle. Dena wondered if that had been when Scott's hair started turning gray. She noticed he didn't wear a wedding ring, so apparently he hadn't remarried.

"It was a long time ago," Scott said. "Thirteen years. I've been through a lot of changes since then. Are you going to be around this week?" he asked, looking directly at Dena.

"Yep. I'm staying with Ham Conklin."

Scott's smile radiated genuine delight. "Me too! It'll be great to get caught up."

Roberta Schuler beckoned to Scott from a nearby knot of people. "Rev, there's someone I want you to meet."

Dena laughed. "'Rev'?"

"That's one of the changes," Scott tossed over his shoulder as he left to greet Roberta. "I'm a Presbyterian minister."

Dena was struck speechless, but Gabe managed, "Wait a minute. Last I heard, he was playing ball for a triple-A team."

"A minister!" she said. "I can't believe it."

"Why? Because he looks like Richard Gere?"

Did she detect a note of petulance? How intriguing. "Well. He doesn't look like any pastor I've ever met."

"And he's staying at Ham's, too," Gabe said. "You'll have all week to get caught up."

"Yes, I'm looking forward to it."

"Or should I say, *we'll* all have a week to get caught up."

Dena stared at him, certain she must have misheard.

No. Ham wouldn't do that to her. He knew what she'd gone through at the end of senior year, knew what Gabe had done, how devastated she'd been. True, Gabe had been as close to Ham as she had, but surely he wouldn't have invited them *both* to share his house this week?

Slowly she said, "Tell me I heard you wrong."

Gabe just smiled and drained his martini glass.

_____ **2** _____

"SHOES LIKE THAT keep guys like me in business."

Dena leaned on the redwood deck railing and
stared far across the lawn at the source of this unsolicited observation. Frank had beached himself
on one of three green-cushioned chaises next to
Ham's large, in-ground swimming pool. The free-
form saltwater pool and the hot tub that jutted from
one side of it were surrounded by a rustic flagstone
apron and so much luxuriant, flowering greenery
that one could easily mistake it for a tropical la-
goon.

Unless one had to share it with Hunky Runkey—
or Chunky Runkey as Dena had begun to think of
him. She glanced at her high-heeled glittery pink
mules, which contrasted nicely with the frosted
green polish on her toenails. "Since when are
neurosurgeons so concerned with feet?"

Frank leaned over to set his breakfast margarita
on the side table. He was dripping wet, wearing a
pair of abbreviated swim trunks he might have
been able to get away with fifteen years and fifty
pounds ago. As he settled back on the chaise with a
grunt, Dena experienced a time warp. She was back
at the Briarfield High cafeteria, staring at the hu-
mongous pan of quivering Jell-O that Mrs. Fagan,

the lunch lady, used to methodically carve into little squares.

Frank snorted. "Who told you I'm a neurosurgeon?"

"That's what you said you were going to be, back in high school."

"Oh. Yeah. Well, I changed my mind."

"And became what instead? An orthopedist?"

"I'm a podiatrist," he said importantly. "A foot doctor."

Dena pushed her sunglasses up her nose. "So if I get a bunion or something this week, I won't have to tear my hair out looking for an emergency all-night podiatrist."

"With shoes like that, bunions should be the least of your worries," he pronounced. "Do you have any ideas what those heels do to your spine?"

She straightened and lazily descended the deck stairs. "No, but I know what they do for my butt. So what happened? Couldn't get into med school?"

Only a princely endowment by Frank Runkey Sr. had gotten Frank Jr. into the third-rate college he'd attended, or so she'd heard.

Frank snatched up his drink, scowling as she reached the stone apron and stepped out of the mules. "At least *I* work on *human* feet. Never had to clip mutts' toenails for a living."

"You should try it sometime. It's very relaxing in a Zen kind of way." She tossed her shades and towel onto one of the other chaises and slipped off her short orange satin robe, revealing a white one-piece swimsuit printed all over with red tulips. Its how-low-can-you-go neckline was cunningly enhanced with underwire, a twentieth-century advancement second only to penicillin in Dena's book.

Frank stared openly as she sauntered to the deep end and stepped onto the diving board. But he wasn't the reason she faltered just as her muscles tensed for the leap. Every nerve ending had gone on red alert—her feminine radar again.

Her gaze was drawn to the redwood deck, where she saw Gabe leaning on the railing precisely where she'd stood not two minutes before. He was wearing khaki shorts and a dark green T-shirt stretched tight in all the right places. She held his gaze for a few moments, until he hid his eyes behind a pair of impenetrably dark sunglasses.

Concentrate, Dena commanded herself. She focused on the crystalline water, on her form and timing, and executed a flawless dive. The cold water swallowed her, surged past her as she bowed her body upward and propelled herself to the surface. She immediately went into a crawl stroke, not pausing when she reached the shallow end where Frank was docked but tucking into a tight racing turn, kicking off the wall, and returning to the deep end, where she tossed her wet hair off her face and began treading water.

Her gaze automatically homed in on the redwood deck, only to find it deserted.

"I forgot what a good swimmer you are," Gabe said, from directly behind her.

Dena turned and squinted up at him, wishing he were more than an indistinct blur looming over her, backlit by the brilliant sunshine. She felt exposed and vulnerable.

She said, "I swim every day."

"Kept up your membership at the Y?"

"I have a pool."

His eyebrows rose. Like Frank, Gabe probably assumed she still groomed dogs for a living. Movement in the corner of her vision drew her attention to Frank, who hoisted his Nimitz-class bulk out of the chaise and slung his towel over a shoulder. He said, "I'm gonna go see if there's any of that French toast left."

Gabe said, "Lunch is in less than an hour."

"I worked up an appetite swimming," Frank said, and set off across the yard to the house.

"How much swimming did he actually do?" Gabe asked, once their housemate was out of earshot.

"I couldn't say. Didn't get to witness that particular spectacle." Dena leaned into a back float and sculled away from Gabe. "You just going to stand there watching, or are you coming in?"

"I'm not wearing trunks."

"You don't need trunks." She glanced toward the house. "No one's watching."

He just stood there. Unable to discern his expression, Dena said, "Maybe it's not such a good idea, after all. Andrea could come out any minute."

"Meaning what?"

"Meaning she might think there's more going on here than a little innocent skinny-dipping."

He crossed his arms. "And why, precisely, should I care what Andrea thinks?"

At the shallow end now, Dena stood. The water came up to her waist. "So come on in, then. The water's perfect."

Gabe stalked to her end of the pool. "I want an

answer. Why do you think something like that would bother Andrea? And why, even if it did, do you imagine I would care?"

She smiled. "You're such a lawyer. Nice to know Daddy's tuition money wasn't wasted."

Obviously Gabe wanted her to believe he and Andrea weren't an item—another too-little-too-late attempt to spare Dena's feelings, most likely. After all, Gabe and Andrea had worked side by side for the past eight years since earning their law degrees from Harvard, their fathers' alma mater. Their mutual attraction was anything but a secret. And, too, most men harbored a special fondness for their first lover, or so it was said.

Neither Gabe nor Andrea had married, which meant they'd probably had some kind of on-again, off-again thing going for fifteen years.

Gabe sighed. "I don't remember you being such a pain in the ass back in high school."

"Are you sure? There must've been some reason you betrayed me."

There. She'd said it. He became very still, very quiet. The seconds ticked by. From the nearby woods came the rustle of small animals, the low hum of insect life.

Quietly he said, "I thought you weren't interested in reasons."

She swallowed hard and looked away. How could it still hurt, after fifteen years? How could she let it twist her insides like this?

She heard movement, and looked up to see Gabe walk around the end of the pool. He stopped at the point closest to her and squatted there, forearms on his thighs. He pulled off his wire-rimmed sunglasses and let them dangle from his long fingers. The sun was no longer behind him, and she saw him clearly.

He said, "Why didn't you let me explain, Dena? Why did you refuse to listen?"

She took a deep breath. "You told me you loved me. I was going to be your first, and you mine." Dena was horrified by the tightness in her throat, the burning in her eyes, but she'd kept the words bottled up for fifteen years, and they wouldn't be stopped now. "We waited, Gabe, and I used to think how beautiful it was going to be when we finally gave ourselves to each other."

"So did I. Dena—"

"And the worst part was, I had to hear about it in school, from Rhonda and Dave and…and everyone. They tripped over themselves, wanting to be the one to tell me. Do you have any idea what that was like?" Gabe must have bragged about his conquest to everyone he knew. The news had spread through the school at light speed.

She hadn't known he could look so miserable, but she rushed on, helpless to stop now that the dam had burst. "You had no problem necking with me in a dark movie theater, or making out in your Camaro at the duck pond, but God forbid your father's snooty colleagues should find out what a low-class girl you were dating. I never even knew the firm was going to have that stupid reception at the country club. You never told me."

"I didn't want you hurt."

"You didn't want to be seen with the *janitor's daughter!* You were too ashamed! So you took Andrea instead. You took her to the reception and you took her out on that damn golf course and you had sex with her there." Dena was breathing hard, trembling with fury and humiliation, as if it had happened yesterday.

Gabe's head was bowed. He gripped the sunglasses so hard it was a wonder they didn't snap. He raised his face and said, "I never tried to excuse what I did, I just wanted to explain. I still do."

"Let me ask you one thing. If I'd done what you did, if I'd snuck around behind your back and dated some other guy, if I'd had sex with him after everything you and I had meant to each other, promised each other…would you have been interested in explanations?"

Gabe's features were rigid, his expression intense. "No," he said at last.

The twinge of satisfaction Dena felt did nothing to assuage the ache in her chest. She'd scratched open an old wound that had never been given a chance to heal, and she wished she'd left it alone.

"There she is," Ham called as he and Scott crossed the lawn toward them. "The Leona Helmsley of the canine world."

Needing a few moments to compose herself, Dena turned and swam the length of the pool. When she surfaced at the deep end, Ham was settling into the chaise abandoned by Frank, and Scott was pulling off the red T-shirt he'd thrown on over black boxer-style trunks. Some kind of marks encircled one of his upper arms, and it took Dena a moment to realize she was looking at a tattoo of a knotted rope.

Good heavens. Reverend Cafferty had a tattoo! She wondered when he'd acquired it—during his days as a minor-league ballplayer probably. She couldn't help noticing, as he strolled to the diving board, that he'd kept himself in shape. She moved out of the line of fire as he launched himself and plunged neatly into the deep water.

Dena swam to the shallow end and climbed out. Gabe was sitting on the edge of a chaise, chatting with Ham, who wore a beat-up panama straw hat, pink plaid Bermuda shorts and a yellow T-shirt with a big, round smiley face on it.

"Ham, we have to talk," she said, grabbing her towel and perching herself on the edge of the third chaise, so that Ham sat between her and Gabe. She glanced toward Scott, swimming laps, and lowered her voice. "You have to know Gabe and I can't both stay here this week."

"Nonsense. There's plenty of room." Ham took a pull from his tumbler of iced coffee and set it on the table.

"I'm not talking about space," she said. "I know the house is big enough."

Ham's father, a third-generation potato farmer, had built the house the year Ham was born. Periodic renovations had never encroached on the original woodwork or the full-length covered front porch, and many of the furnishings Ham's mother had chosen eighty years ago were still in use. It was the ideal setting for a bed-and-breakfast inn.

Dena continued, "Ham, you're very generous to open up your home to us. But you know what happened between me and Gabe. To be frank, I have no desire to share a house with him for a week."

Gabe drawled, "Personally, I don't see the problem, Dena."

"I need you here," Ham insisted. "Both of you. It's been such a relief to me, knowing you'd be here to help oversee everything...now that I'm not up to it." He placed a liver-spotted hand on his chest, and Dena felt a jolt of alarm.

"Ham, what is it? Your heart?" She glanced at Gabe, who shrugged, wide-eyed. "I didn't know you were...having difficulty. Why didn't you tell us?"

He waved negligently. "Ah, why bother everyone else with my troubles? I'll be fine as long as I take it easy. And don't get too worked up."

Dena bit her lip, wondering how to proceed. "The thing is, Ham, I'm just not comfortable in this situation. If I'd known you invited Gabe... Anyway, I'm sure he can give you all the help you need around here. I'm going to get a hotel room."

Ham jerked upright on the chaise, his expression stricken. "But there's so much to be done. I've been counting on you, Dena. I can't rely on the others."

Gabe placed a reassuring hand on Ham's shoulder, urging him to lean back. Ham slumped wearily, exhaustion warring with agitation on his expressive face.

Dena knew Gabe was as worried as she. He kept his expression carefully bland, but his anxiety was evident, at least to her. Ham had never been one to panic like this, for no good reason. She didn't want to think of her old friend suffering mental or physical frailty, but he was eighty years old, after all.

Gabe sent Dena a pointed look. "Everything will be fine, Ham. No need to worry. Dena and I will both be here for you."

How dare he speak for her! "I still don't see why

it's necessary for us both to stay," she said. "What exactly do you need done, Ham?"

He patted his pockets distractedly. "Oh, the shopping. And running people around to all these reunion activities. You two brought your cars. The others...they flew in."

She said, "Well, in that case, I'm sure Gabe can—"

"Seven people in the house!" he fretted. "I'll never manage with seven people!"

Gabe said gently, "Ham, there are eight of us altogether."

"What?"

Dena did a quick count. "Gabe's right. Him and me, you and Reba, Scott, Frank, Rhonda, and Andrea. That's eight."

"Frank? Who's Frank?" Ham's eyes darted around; he had a death grip on the arms of the chaise. "I don't know any Frank!"

"Frank Runkey," Gabe said. "An old student of yours. He lives in Minnesota now and you invited him to stay here this week. Didn't you?"

"I don't know any Frank!"

"Sure you do," Dena said soothingly. She placed her hand over his. "He sat next to you at breakfast this morning."

"I don't know any Frank!"

Dena looked imploringly at Gabe.

"They, uh, used to call him Hunky," Gabe offered.

Ham bolted upright again, eyes bulging with outrage. "Hunky Runkey's staying here? Who told him he could?"

"I was wondering the same thing," Gabe muttered.

"I believe his mother is a friend of Reba's," Dena said. "You invited him as a favor to her. Isn't that right?"

"Reba?" Ham blinked in confusion. He patted his pockets again.

"What are you looking for?" Gabe asked.

"My pills. They're not here."

"I'll be happy to stay," Dena said quickly. "So will Gabe. Don't worry about a thing, Ham. Everything's under control."

Ham leaned back with a gusty sigh. "I knew you wouldn't let me down."

Gabe said, "I'll go get your pills if you tell me where they are."

Ham waved off his concern. "I'm fine now. It passed."

Gabe caught Dena's eye, and she read his silent gratitude. With the barest nod she conceded the necessity to put their own preferences on hold, for Ham's sake. It was a small price to pay for their old friend's health and peace of mind.

We're doing it again! she realized. Communicating without words, flawlessly deciphering each other's slightest change in expression. Just as they'd done last night when she first encountered Frank. Just as they used to do back when she thought the sun rose and set on Gabriel Moreau.

A splashing sound drew Dena's attention to the pool. Scott levered himself out of the shallow end, and with a start she wondered how long he'd been standing there and how much he'd overheard. Not that everyone didn't know what had happened fifteen years ago, but that was fifteen years ago, and she had no desire to make her private life public yet again.

He quickly toweled off and sat against the raised end of the chaise Dena occupied, propping a leg behind her. She started to get up.

"Sit," Scott ordered. "There's room for both of us. So what's with the Leona Helmsley comparison? Can I assume you're no longer Going to the Dogs?" he asked, referring to the dog-grooming business she'd worked for part-time during high school and full-time after graduation.

"I worked there for five years," Dena said, "while I lived at home, put in all the overtime I could, and saved every nickel. And I'd started breeding pugs and selling them. All so I could start my own business."

"Let me guess," Scott said, with a beguiling grin. "Could this business possibly be related to dogs?" Her love of canines had never been a secret.

"Dena's a real go-getter," Ham put in. "She saw a need and addressed it. And look at her now!"

"Pet owners never like having to board their dogs and cats when they go on vacation," Dena said. "They feel guilty. Kennels can be so dreary. So I came up with an idea for a pet hotel. Real swanky, with all the comforts of home. Private apartments, a huge yard and plenty of personalized attention from the staff."

Scott laughed. "No kidding. What do you call it, the Waldog Astoria?"

"Xanadu Pet Resort. I just opened the sixth one, in Litchfield, Connecticut."

"Xanadu? That's yours?" Gabe's astonishment was delicious to behold. "I don't believe it!"

"Why? Did you think I was going to spend my entire life giving poodle cuts at Going to the Dogs?"

"No, no, of course not," he said, obviously forgetting she could read his thoughts like a billboard.

"As I recall, we used to talk about our goals, you and I. More than once I mentioned that I wanted to start my own business."

"Well, maybe you did," he mumbled. "It was a long time ago."

Gabe could pretend he'd suffered a memory lapse, but Dena knew he'd simply discounted her aspirations as adolescent dreams. Wishful thinking. Whereas his own future plans had been carved in stone from an early age. He'd have been indignant if she'd expressed doubt in his ability to follow through on those plans. In this, as in the freedom he'd felt to cheat on her, the old double standard was alive and well.

She made no attempt to school her expression, openly inviting him to follow the direction of her thoughts. He held her gaze for a few moments and looked away.

"Six pet hotels," Scott said. "You must be raking it in."

"I'm doing better than I'd hoped. You'd be surprised how much people will pay to be relieved of guilt where their pets are concerned. They want Fido to have as much fun on vacation as they do."

"Dena's one of Briarfield's proudest success stories," Ham said, "a wonderful role model for the current crop of students, especially the girls. She's gone into the school a couple of times to talk to the kids about what it takes to make something of yourself. Namely, sacrifice, perseverance and good old-fashioned elbow grease—concepts some of them seem to have a hard time grasping in this era of instant gratification."

"Better watch it," Gabe said, with a tender smile. "You're beginning to sound like an old fogy."

"I don't know about that," Scott said. "Nowadays the idea of hard work is considered downright radical."

"Listen to us," Dena said. "We've turned into our parents." She held Gabe's gaze for an extra beat, until a subtle narrowing of his eyes told her that her remark had struck home.

The entire time she and Gabe had dated, Lucien and Cynthia Moreau had done everything in their power to break them up—especially Lucien, who'd actively lobbied for a union between his son and Andrea Pittman, the daughter of his law partner. Gabe's father had envisioned the marriage as some sort of glorious dynastic merger.

Gabe's relationship with Dena had caused his parents no end of grief. She wasn't "suitable." She wasn't from their lofty socioeconomic stratum. That Gabe had defied his parents and refused to give her up had reinforced Dena's romantically naive assumption that theirs was a meeting of soul mates, a match destined to last a lifetime.

Gabe had been born into an affluent life-style completely alien to her: the money, the servants, the lavish trips to Europe, the gated estate she'd dubbed Château Moreau. He'd exhibited a confidence and sense of entitlement that had made him seem older, more sophisticated, than his years.

Dena, on the other hand, had lived in a ramshackle rented bungalow on the proverbial wrong side of the tracks, with her parents, four siblings and her beloved black pugs, Mildred and Horace. Her dad had worked as a janitor in the Briarfield school system until two years ago, when severe back problems had finally forced him out on disability. Her mom had quit her job as a nursing-home aide and they'd retired to Maine, with some financial assistance from Dena and her two older brothers.

She and Gabe were from different worlds, but it hadn't mattered because they'd been young and in love, and when you're young and in love, you can make anything happen, as long as you're together.

At least that was what they'd told each other. Until the moment of truth when Gabe had taken Andrea out on that golf course, and Dena had learned that no matter how hard she tried, no matter how much love she had to give, she'd always be "the janitor's daughter," as his parents used to refer to her—too tawdry, too lowbrow, too déclassé to ever fit into Gabe Moreau's rarefied world.

The yawning emptiness had taken a long time to heal, but eventually it had and she'd moved on. Nevertheless, she often found herself wondering how different her life would have been, if only…

If only Gabe had shown more moral fiber. If only she'd been the kind of girl he'd wanted and needed. So many ifs.

Was Gabe turning into his father, as she'd so spitefully implied? Thus far, Dena saw scant evidence to the contrary, and it saddened her. All things considered, perhaps it was for the best that things hadn't worked out between them.

The sound of Andrea Pittman's cultured, slightly nasal voice yanked Dena out of her reverie. "Sorry I missed everybody at breakfast. I'm not trying to be unsociable, I just had a ton of paperwork to get caught up on. I rarely eat breakfast anyway."

Andrea wore an elegant black one-piece with gold accents that matched her gold leather sandals, delicate neck chain, and understated earrings. A sheer floral chiffon pareo was tied around her slender hips. Andrea was five foot two and a hundred pounds at the most. Everything about her was petite and perfectly formed, from her slim thighs to her tiny feet to her impossibly narrow waist, which Gabe could probably span with his hands.

Her dark hair was cut in a very short yet feminine style, feathery around the face and nape. Her eyes were pale silver gray, set off with a minimum of makeup. An impeccable French manicure adorned her nails. Andrea Pittman was as sleek and polished as a strand of pearls.

Next to her, Dena felt more like the macaroni necklace she'd made for her mother in kindergarten.

A smile tugged at her mouth. Mom, God bless her, had put that string of painted wagon-wheel pasta around her neck and worn it to church with her best Sunday outfit.

In truth, Dena had long ago come to terms with her size. She'd never be five foot two, which was just as well, considering her fondness for good food and hearty portions. The surplus vertical inches helped keep the surplus horizontal inches off her ample but shapely figure. Her active life-style didn't hurt, either.

Ignoring the pool, Andrea said, "As long as we're all sharing," and moved to join Gabe on his chaise.

Dena bristled at the reference to sharing. Was that what Andrea had been doing fifteen years ago? *Sharing* Dena's boyfriend? Funny. She'd always thought that was called *stealing*.

Andrea lifted Dena's neon-aqua, rhinestone-studded cat's-eye sunglasses from the chaise to avoid parking her itty-bitty butt on them. "My God, whose are these?"

As if there could be any doubt. Which didn't stop Scott from saying, "Oh, so that's where I left them." He plucked them out of Andrea's hand and put them on. He looked ridiculous and adorable and perfectly at ease.

Ham said, "Where can I get a pair?"

Andrea turned to Dena. "I have to hand it to you, wearing shades like that. I wouldn't have the nerve. But then, you've always had your own unique sense of style."

Gabe glanced at Dena, as if to assess her reaction to this backhanded compliment. The old Dena would have been too embarrassed and flustered to respond. The old Dena hadn't yet learned to take pride in her "unique sense of style."

"Funny, you putting it that way," Dena said, "that you wouldn't have the nerve. Which only goes to show, audacious behavior is in the eye of the beholder."

An experienced lawyer, Andrea kept her expression neutral. Only her heightened color and the muscle tic near her eye revealed that Dena's none-too-subtle jab had hit its mark.

Glancing at Gabe, Dena saw the same secret little smile he'd worn last night when she'd put Frank and Dave in their place.

Say goodbye to the old Dena.

"Well." Ham slapped the arms of his chaise. "If I don't get hopping in the kitchen, I'll have to run out to the burger place."

"You?" Gabe asked, rising with him. "Patronizing an exploitative, bloodsucking multinational corporation? I don't believe it."

"You ever taste that Humongo Supreme? With double cheese?"

"Don't tell me you eat that stuff?" Dena asked, gathering her things and joining Ham and Gabe on the walk back to the house. "What about your heart condition?"

"Ah, once in a while won't make a difference," Ham said. "Speaking of grilled flesh, Rhonda made out a shopping list for tonight's cookout on the beach. You two don't mind running out to the supermarket after lunch, do you?"

"Well, no," Dena said. "What about Rhonda? Doesn't she want to come with us?"

"I need her here."

He left it at that, and all Dena could say was, "Sure. We'll go shopping. No problem."

"Whatever we can do to help," Gabe seconded.

"In that case, you can start by giving me a hand in the kitchen," Ham said as he ascended the deck steps.

"We'll be right in." Gabe grabbed Dena's elbow to hold her back. "In a minute."

When the door had closed after Ham, Gabe said, "I'm worried about him."

"So am I, but there's something I don't get. This place is an active bed-and-breakfast inn. Ham often has all three upstairs rooms filled. That's six extra people right there if it's couples, and sometimes there are kids, too."

"So?"

"So why is he all of a sudden freaking out over a few guests?"

"Well…maybe he feels an increased responsibility because we're honest-to-God invited guests, not the paying kind."

"Did you know he was having trouble with his heart?"

"Not until today."

She sighed. "Damn it. I don't want him to get old."

Gabe smiled gently. "It's a little late for that. He was getting on in years when we first met him. He retired the year we graduated, remember?"

"Well, I don't have to like it." Ham had been like a grandfather to both of them—though their real grandfathers hadn't been nearly so eccentric, iconoclastic or opinionated. Ham had been so certain, back then, that Dena and Gabe belonged together, had tried so hard to mend the rift, or at least to get them talking. Always the idealist.

"I know you'd rather be anywhere else this week, Dena." Gabe glanced toward the pool area, where Andrea sunned herself while Scott swam. "This has got to be uncomfortable as hell for you, what with Andrea staying here, too." He sighed. "She sort of wangled an invitation, and I didn't know you'd be here."

"Yes, well, I don't want to cramp your style. If you two want to share a room or anything, just pretend I'm not here."

Gabe scowled. "What makes you think we have something going on?"

Dena let her raised eyebrows say it all.

He looked off into the distance for a moment. When he spoke, his voice reflected frustration and more than a little resentment. "Not that I'm trying to force any *unwanted explanations* on you, but for your information, Andrea and I are work colleagues only. End of story. We haven't been anything more since that night fifteen years ago."

Dena didn't know whether to believe him, given their history. "You're assuming I care. Your personal life doesn't concern me, Gabe. Let's just try to get through the next week with a minimum of excitement. Then, if we're lucky, we won't have to deal with each other for another fifteen years."

3

"YOU CAN SET THAT DOWN right here," Rhonda said. "Thanks, Gabe."

He positioned the huge cooler chest, loaded with ice and bottles of beer and soda, on the sand near the wooden picnic table Rhonda indicated. She shook out a plastic red-and-white-checked tablecloth, and he helped her position it. His gaze kept straying to the nearby volleyball game. No sooner had he volunteered to be the designated pack animal than the game had started.

Figures, he grumbled to himself.

"So forty-one people are going to be around for the whole week, including spouses, and a lot of them are local," Rhonda said, smoothing out the plastic. "Of course, most of the locals have to go to work, so our daytime events won't be as well attended as the evening ones. My Don would've stayed if he could've gotten the time off, but the senior guys get the pick of vacation time, so he had to go back to Cincinnati. Would you put stacks of paper plates on the corners? The breeze is blowing the tablecloth up."

Gabe obliged, one eye on the volleyball court. He caught occasional glimpses of a headful of pale blond curls, and long, long legs emerging from short, short cutoffs. Dena's snug, sleeveless, white

T-shirt had been tie-dyed aquamarine, making it appear, from a distance, as if her torso had been painted to resemble a cloudy sky. Like the other players, she was barefoot.

Rhonda had chosen a South Shore beach for this cookout, and the longer drive had been worth it. Instead of the ubiquitous rocks and tame waters of Long Island Sound on the North Shore, they were frolicking in fine white sand against the backdrop of the raucous Atlantic. Gabe filled his lungs with the brine-scented ocean breeze. Overhead, screeching seagulls wheeled against a brilliant azure sky.

"Luckily Don can set his hours," Rhonda continued, "so there's no problem getting the kids off to school, and a neighbor will pick them up and keep them till he gets home at six. Did you buy the heavy-duty foil? I want to cover the grills, they look kind of icky, and the regular foil won't—"

"I'm not sure," he lied, having watched Dena javelin-toss a long roll of heavy-duty foil into their shopping cart at the Waldbaum's supermarket earlier in the day. "I'd better go check."

Grabbing a beer from the cooler, Gabe made his escape, hiding out on the far side of the volleyball court where Rhonda wouldn't be likely to spot him. Dena, in center forward position, appeared absorbed in the game, passing the ball and returning volleys with a joyous enthusiasm that made her seem eighteen again.

Seemingly oblivious to Gabe's presence on the sidelines, she leaped to spike the ball over the net, successfully firing it into the sand at her opponents' feet to score the winning point. She shared a triumphant hoot and a spontaneous hug with Scott Cafferty, playing left forward.

"Devlin's got the moves!" Scott hollered, giving her a congratulatory whack on the rump.

Most of the players, including Dena, wandered off the court as a handful of diehards tried to drum up interest in another game. Dena was flushed, breathing hard, and Gabe's first thought was that this was how she must look after sex.

No, not quite, he decided. Her smile would be a tad dreamier, her hair a bit more mussed, her green eyes slumberous.

But you'll never know for sure.

Succumbing to an impulse, Gabe caught Dena's eye and wagged his frosty beer bottle invitingly. Her steps slowed. Her expression turned wary as she approached him. He held out his beer to her, knowing she had to be thirsty, silently daring her to turn it down. She stared at the bottle, three-fourths full, and finally took it from him.

As Gabe watched her take a long swallow, he felt he'd achieved a small victory. There had been a time when he and Dena had shared everything, from bottles of Dr. Brown's black-cherry soda, to the Nestlé's Crunch bars they'd both craved, to the pizza they'd ordered at Carlucci's every Friday night without fail, topped with anchovies and fried eggplant. No one else had been able to appreciate the appeal of anchovies and eggplant, but so what? No one and nothing else had mattered, as long as he and Dena were together.

She handed him the beer, and he took a sip as he placed his hand on her back to steer her toward the water. She stiffened slightly, prompting him to let his hand linger a few more seconds. If Reverend Cafferty of the movie-star hair and the ball-player's build and the *tattoo*, of all things, could hug her and give her a friendly slap on the bottom, then Gabe could damn well touch her back. He paused on the boardwalk to set down his beer and remove his sandals.

Dena glanced over her shoulder. "We should be helping Rhonda."

"Yeah, you sound real enthusiastic about that," he said dryly, as they started shuffling through the sand. "Don't worry, Rhonda Peterson's never had a problem recruiting 'volunteers.' You didn't come to this reunion to be at that woman's beck and call." The sun was slipping into the western sky, casting long shadows and gilding Dena's skin and wind-whipped hair. "Why *did* you come to this reunion?"

She shrugged. "For the same reason you did, I suppose."

I wouldn't be that lucky.

"To see the old gang," she said. "Get caught up."

"Or to let everyone see you no longer groom dogs for a living?"

She shot him a hard look. "You think I came to brag about my accomplishments?"

"Why not? It's why most of these people are here. To rub everyone else's nose in their success. Ginger Steadman carries around this little photo album with pictures of her summer place in the Hamptons, with the his and hers matching Beamers out front. Making sure everyone knows she married the liposuction king of Park Avenue. To hear her tell it, this guy's trimmed more thighs than Frank Perdue."

"I don't need to prove anything to anyone."

"Maybe not," he said, "but I don't mind telling you, I'm impressed. Never knew you had it in you."

"I know." Her tone was flat, resigned.

He studied her profile, silently urging her to look at him. When she didn't, he said, "I can't get anything right, can I?"

They came to a stop, having reached the water's edge. The sand under their feet was wet and studded with shells and sea-tossed stones. A wave rumbled ashore and receded, just missing their toes.

Dena stared fixedly at the ocean. When she spoke, her voice was strained. "It shouldn't matter. Not anymore. Not after everything else."

He wanted to reach out, to touch her, soothe her. Instead her said, "What shouldn't matter?"

"I thought we knew each other so well. Back then. It was almost…almost as if we could read each other's minds."

He swallowed hard. "I remember."

"But we never did know each other, not really."

"Dena. Look at me."

She closed her eyes briefly, shook her head as if trying to dislodge a persistent tune from her mind. She took a deep breath and raised her face to his, and in that instant as he looked into her eyes, Gabe knew she was right.

This wasn't the Dena he thought he knew. That Dena used to gaze at him with perfect adoration, making him feel like there was nothing he couldn't do, no worlds he couldn't conquer. That Dena had never looked at him with this cool implacability.

She said, "Did you think you were the only one with aspirations?"

His first impulse was to spout another pat denial. But then something broke loose inside him, and he said, "Yes. I guess I did. I was young and stupid. And arrogant."

His candid response seemed to throw her off balance. "Imagine that," she murmured with a little smile, "an arrogant eighteen-year-old."

"As far as I was concerned, the future was this bright, wonderful place where I'd work hard and plug myself in to this great life I had all planned out. If I thought of your future at all, I guess I saw it as sort of—well, as an extension of mine. You had these big dreams, but to me, they were just that, because I figured we'd always be together."

There was that trademark lopsided smile, more cynical than amused. "And in your bright, wonderful future, I would've been tickled pink just to be a member of the team: Mrs. Gabriel Moreau, Esquire."

"Like I said, young and stupid."

"And arrogant."

"I believe we've established that."

Dena studied him, her expression solemn. "Thank you, Gabe. For your honesty."

He shrugged. "What have I got to lose at this point?"

She didn't even try to answer that, but started walking along the shoreline toward the lowering sun, partly concealed by thin stratus clouds tinged pink and apricot. Gabe fell into step beside her. The aromas of charcoal-grilled burgers and hot dogs drifted from the picnic area.

"Do you still like sunsets?" he asked.

"I don't think that's something you ever stop liking."

He used to pick up Dena after school—to do their homework at the library, or so they'd told her parents. He'd park the Camaro someplace where they could watch the sunset, usually the local duck pond, and they'd neck and pet until he thought he'd explode.

Their pants had always remained zipped, at her insistence, but he'd discovered there was a heck of a lot you could do with your pants zipped. They'd planned to make love for the first time after the senior prom, and Gabe had purchased condoms five months in advance.

As it happened, neither of them had attended the prom. Gabe's parents, oblivious to the Golf Course Incident and the havoc it had wreaked on his life, had urged him to escort Andrea. Such a nice, sweet, suitable girl, they'd insisted. She and Gabe had so much in common. Why didn't he ask her on a second date?

As for Dena, even if someone else had invited her to the prom, Gabe could only assume she'd been too humiliated to attend, having become an object of ridicule, thanks to him.

"Why haven't you ever married?" she asked.

"Why haven't you?"

"Objection, Your Honor. Witness is evading the question."

"And here I was hoping to get away from the courtroom for a week." Gabe reached down and picked up a flat black stone, about the size of his thumb tip. He turned it over in his fingers, let its cool smoothness center him.

"Isn't that part of your master plan," Dena asked, "along with the partnership and the sprawling home in Greenwich? An ornamental wife, two point three kids—"

"And the family dog that we'd board at Xanadu so we wouldn't have to feel guilty."

She chuckled—a coup! "Precisely."

"It's the old story," he said. "I never met the right woman. And the sprawling home in Greenwich is a sprawling apartment."

"I know. I saw the photo spread in *New England Accents.*"

He grimaced. "My mother's handiwork. She brought in her decorator. It isn't the way I would've fixed the place up."

"Then why didn't you?"

"What?"

"Fix the place up yourself."

"Who has time?"

"Some people make time. So Mom is furnishing your home, and Dad is calling the shots at work. Why do I get the feeling not much has changed in your life?"

The way Gabe figured it, Dena was entitled to get in a few punches. Still, he felt compelled to point out the obvious. "There's more to life than what kind of sofa you sit on and how many billable hours you put in each week."

The breeze blew her hair across her face, and she pushed it back. He had the feeling she wanted to ask him to elaborate, but she remained silent.

"How are Mimi and Carl doing?" he asked, referring to Dena's parents.

"They retired to southern Maine two years ago. Dad's back got too bad for him to keep working."

"I always liked your folks. Tell them I said hi."

She nodded.

"Or maybe you shouldn't. Do they know what happened? Why we broke up?"

"No." Dena's voice was tight. "I never told them."

Gabe should have known. He'd spent weeks looking over his shoulder fifteen years ago, dreading a confrontation with Carl Devlin and his three strapping sons, a confrontation that never materialized.

"So," Gabe said. "Is there anyone special at the moment?"

"Not at the moment."

He felt a glimmer of satisfaction until she added, "I almost got married four years ago."

He tossed the black stone into the waves. "What happened?"

"I caught him cheating on me."

He studied her face for some hint that she was joking. She wasn't.

She gave a nonchalant shrug. "Maybe it's me."

Gabe stopped walking. Dena took another few steps and glanced over her shoulder.

"It isn't you," he said. "Don't ever think that."

She stared at him, and in her eyes he read the crushing self-doubt she kept carefully hidden from the world. He'd helped put that self-doubt there, and the knowledge shamed him. He moved to close the distance between them as a wave broke and icy seawater surged over their feet. Dena flinched as if burned, and stepped back onto dry sand. The fleeting connection they'd shared vanished in the blink of an eye, as fragile as sea foam.

She looked at him, the impassive mask once more in place. "I told you, you don't know me. You never did."

Then let's start over, he wanted to say, but she was gone, striding swiftly across the beach toward the picnic area.

4

THE WINERY TOUR GUIDE, a rangy man in his mid-fifties named Ted, led the group into the cellar room where wine was aged. An agreeable sweet-musty aroma filled the cool, windowless space, crammed with sealed wooden barrels stacked on their sides. Those nearest Dena jostled her as the eighteen people in their party tried to get near enough to hear the guide expound on the type of wood used for barrels and the length of time various wines were allowed to age.

Dena heard the muted ringing of a phone, and turned to see Andrea, at the rear of the crowd, fish her cell phone out of her shoulder bag. Andrea turned her back and kept her voice low; nevertheless, her side of the conversation was clearly audible.

"You're missing a terrific morning, Gabe. We've already been to two wineries and I don't know how many antique shops. If you'd brought those files out with you Saturday, you wouldn't have had to go back for them. You know what they say—the memory's the first thing to go." After a moment she laughed. "Okay, the second thing."

Dena felt a stab of irritation listening to Andrea banter with Gabe. They were work colleagues only, he'd claimed. Dena still found that hard to believe, although she had to admit he'd been surprisingly candid yesterday evening during their walk on the beach—endearingly candid, she thought with a half smile.

Which didn't mean he was above skirting the truth when it suited him, she reminded herself. He was, after all, a consummate lawyer.

At the very least, Gabe and Andrea must have developed a warm friendship over the years, having attended Harvard together before joining the family firm, where they presumably worked closely on cases. The fact that their fathers had been best buddies since childhood, and law partners for thirty years, meant Gabe and Andrea no doubt saw a lot of each other outside the firm as well.

"You sound like you're calling from the road," Andrea said. "Well, floor it! We'll save a place for you at lunch. Our reservation's for one-thirty." She gave him the name of the restaurant and directions, and returned the phone to her bag.

From the cellar the group moved on to the favorite part of any winery tour, the tasting. They crowded around the bar in the tasting room as Ted poured a modest amount of pale wine into eighteen wineglasses. He explained that they'd be sampling six wines, starting with the lightest white and ending with a robust cabernet. The first offering was dreadful, and Dena was grateful for the basket of bland crackers sitting on the bar.

As Ted poured the next selection, a chardonnay, he explained that wine is meant to be drunk with meals rather than on its own, because of how it reacts with the carbohydrates in food. Dena felt a sharp tap on her shoulder and turned to see Andrea beaming up at her. She'd been doing that all morning, catching her eye, smiling at her—as if they were the best of pals!

"I've been waiting for a chance to chat with you," Andrea said. "To kind of, you know, get caught up."

As Dena grappled for a response, Andrea tugged her arm, urging her away from the crowd toward a quiet corner where wine paraphernalia was displayed for sale.

"Trust me," Andrea said, "You don't want to try any more of those wines. This vineyard is far from the best Long Island has to offer. I *love* this, by the way," she added, plucking at Dena's short white sundress, embellished with appliquéd images of cats and dogs.

"I'll make one for you," Dena said.

"What?"

"I decorated it myself. I'll do one for you in your size."

"Oh…that's not…I couldn't possibly let you go to so much—"

"No trouble at all." With a straight face Dena added, "Throw a dark blazer over it and you can wear it to the firm."

That muscle twitched near Andrea's eye again, even as her grin stretched wider. "You're just…the same sweet, generous Dena, aren't you?" she gushed. "I can't tell you how many times I've meant to pick up the phone and give you a call, but, well, you know how it is. Life just happens, and before you know it, fifteen years have passed!"

"Gosh, Andrea, I haven't thought about calling you at all," Dena said pleasantly. "Not even once."

Andrea's strained chuckle was followed by, "Well, you see? We all get so caught up in our work. Speaking of which, I heard about your string of pet resorts." She gave Dena a playful shove. "Who'd have thought our Dena had it in her?"

"No one, it would seem."

"From dog groomer to owner of a business enterprise worth five point three million dollars and growing! I'm telling you, I nearly collapsed in shock."

"Me, I'm not so easily shocked," Dena said. "For example, it doesn't surprise me at all that you lost no time finding out what Xanadu is worth."

"I knew you wouldn't mind, savvy businesswoman that you are. Now, I'm going to ask you straight out," Andrea said, spreading her palms, "and feel free to tell me to go to hell. But are you happy with your current legal representation?"

"Go to hell, Andrea."

"Because I'll be honest with you, and this is advice I'd give my own mother. The firm you're using—Gilliam, Shapiro and Manning—is a fine one, Harry Manning is a real smart lawyer—"

"Yes, he's done very well for me."

"—but every firm has its weak points, and I'm not trying to run down Gilliam, Shapiro, but between you and me—and this is something you might not know, not being an insider as it were— but their track record for companies like yours—"

"Andrea?"

"Yes?"

"Tell me you're not trying to get me to switch my business to your firm."

Andrea smiled indulgently. "I've seen it before,

you know, when a moneymaking idea takes off unexpectedly, and an inexperienced entrepreneur suddenly finds herself struggling to cope with rapid expansion, site acquisition, tax repercussions, all kinds of liability.... It's all too easy to make the wrong decisions, trust the wrong people. At Moreau Pittman we—"

Dena made a "time-out" T with her hands. "Okay. As for my 'unexpected' success. Let me share with you Dena Devlin's First Rule of Business: If your success comes as a surprise, you don't have any business *being* in business. It's not a game where you try this thing and that thing willy-nilly and hope that something takes off. You have to do your homework and *know* it's going to take off before you commit your time, assets, and energy."

"Well, there's no question—"

"I'm not finished. As for inexperienced little me struggling to cope with the 'suddenness' of it all— I've worked for fifteen years to get where I am now. Days, nights, weekends, holidays. When you were still in law school, I was opening my second location."

"Oh, I know how hard you must've—"

"Did you discuss this with Gabe?" Dena asked.

"Well, naturally we talked it over. Bringing new business into the firm is a priority for us both."

Dena's stomach clenched, and it had nothing to do with the lousy wine. Gabe had come across as so sincere, so candid—*endearingly* candid! And why not? He'd been actively wooing a prospective client. He and his law partner had discussed Dena and Xanadu, had no doubt strategized about what it would take to win her trust and get her to switch to their firm.

Dena heard Ted wrapping up the tasting and inviting everyone to peruse the merchandise and the wines offered for sale. She moved closer to Andrea and, keeping her voice low, said, "Listen carefully, because I don't want any misunderstandings. I will never give my business to your firm. Don't ask again."

Andrea sighed. "Is this about what happened when we were kids?"

Dena shifted closer still, forcing the smaller woman to back up into a display table. "You slept with my boyfriend, Andrea."

"We were *kids!* Don't you think it's time to move on—"

"It wasn't enough that you had everything I could only dream of having. The money. The house. The clothes. It wasn't enough that you had every boy in school drooling over you. You could've had anyone you wanted, but you had to take the one guy I loved. We were going to be married."

An ugly blush mottled Andrea's cheeks. "Just to set the record straight—and I'm only saying this so we can get it out in the open and get past it—Gabe wasn't acting like someone contemplating marriage. When he asked me out I questioned why he wasn't taking you, and he said something to the effect that you were out of the equation. Which I took to mean you two were no longer seeing each other."

Dena found it depressingly easy to imagine eighteen-year-old Gabe asking Andrea to that law-firm affair, saying those things. *Don't worry about Dena.*

She's out of the equation. So sure of himself. So arrogant.

She took a slow, deep breath. *It was a long time ago*, she told herself. *He means nothing to you now.*

Andrea placed a sisterly hand on Dena's arm. In a just-between-us-gals tone she said, "Believe me, I didn't go to that country-club reception thinking *that* was going to happen. But even back then, Gabe could be very, well, *persuasive.* I'm sure you know what I mean."

Dena did indeed know what she meant. She herself had managed to resist his seductive "persuasiveness" and insisted they wait until the senior prom to consummate their relationship. After she'd learned what had happened between him and Andrea, she was glad she hadn't succumbed to him.

Andrea, however, had succumbed on that long-ago night on the golf course, and probably not for the last time. Her offhand reference to "even back then" prompted Dena to mentally fill in the part left unsaid: Even back then, *just as now*, Gabe Moreau was an accomplished seducer.

People were beginning to drift out to their cars. As Dena prepared to join them, she said to Andrea, "Some people may consider 'ethical lawyer' to be a contradiction in terms, but let me assure you, I require some degree of honor in anybody I do business with. You and your *partner* aren't even in the running."

5

GABE LEANED BACK from the worktable and rubbed his burning eyes. He'd been going over files on the Beckman case for nearly three hours and he could no longer concentrate on the words before him. He hadn't wanted to miss the winery-and-antiques trip that morning, but once he'd decided to stay out here for the whole week, he'd had no choice but to drive to the office in Manhattan and pick up work that couldn't wait until next Monday. On his way back he'd made a detour to Greenwich, Connecticut, to stuff a week's worth of clothes into a suitcase.

He'd arrived at the restaurant late and found that Andrea, familiar with his preferences, had already ordered lunch for him. She'd saved a place next to herself at the long banquette table that had been set up for their group. Dena had sat at the opposite end from them. Every time he'd tried to catch her eye she'd coldly ignored him. He wouldn't have thought she'd still be miffed after their chat on the beach, but he could think of no other explanation for her hostility.

You don't know me, she'd said. *You never did.*

Was it true? Gabe wondered. Had he been so self-absorbed in high school, so wrapped up in his own needs and goals, that he hadn't bothered to really get to know the girl he'd been in love with—the girl he'd expected to spend the rest of his life with?

I'm not the same stupid kid, he wanted to tell her.

An irresistible aroma drifted through the open windows facing the backyard—beef brisket being slowly smoked over glowing chunks of hickory in a cylindrical water smoker. Ham had massaged a spicy dry rub into the ten-pound slab of meat last night. He'd started smoking it that morning while everyone else had been on the winery excursion, basting it with a tangy, tomato-based "mop" that included a healthy portion of Kentucky bourbon. The brisket had been slow-cooking for six hours so far; according to Ham's earlier prediction, it would need another two to three hours.

The room Gabe was using wasn't a bedroom at all, but Ham's workshop, a spacious, free-standing room set off the back deck and accessed through a breezeway. Gabe had had to clear power tools and scraps of lumber off the scarred plywood-and-sawhorse worktable in order to spread out his files.

Sunlight poured in through overhead skylights and multipaned windows on three sides, highlighting every bump and nick in the white plaster walls and worn plank flooring. A smaller storage room abutted the fourth wall. Metal shelving units stood along the perimeter of the room, filled with tools, cans of paint, gardening supplies, and jars of nails, screws and small hardware.

Ham and Reba shared a comfortable master suite on the first floor of the house. The male guests had gallantly offered the ladies use of the three second-floor bedrooms, though Frank had grumbled about having to bunk down on the convertible sofa bed in the living room. Scott had cheerfully claimed the finished basement rec room with its futon, which left the workshop for Gabe. He didn't mind. A roll-away cot had been placed in one corner, and there was a bathroom off the utility room across the breezeway. What more did he need?

Okay, he knew what more he needed, or at least desperately wanted, but there wasn't much chance of that happening this week. Besides, the two of them would never fit on that dinky cot.

The Beckman case. Concentrate on the damn Beckman case, he commanded himself, and flipped open a folder with enough force to cause the whole thing to fly off the worktable and onto the floor, scattering papers.

With a muttered curse, Gabe abandoned the steel folding chair and squatted on the floor to scoop up the pages. He heard the door open, heard brisk footfalls crossing the room, but the table was in the way and all he could make out was bare feminine legs ending in high-heeled clear plastic sandals with big white and yellow daisies centered over the insteps.

He emerged from behind the table. Dena screamed and clutched her heart.

"I have that effect on women," he said.

"What—what are you doing here?"

Dropping the folder on the table, he spread his arms wide. "Be it ever so humble."

"You're staying *here?*" Her gaze took in the cluttered workroom, lingering on the little bed, its sheets and blanket in a jumble.

"Where did you think I was sleeping the last two

nights?" he asked, knowing if she answered "Andrea's room," he'd blow a gasket.

"Well, I didn't really know, but I figured it was somewhere in the house. Not the shed."

"Workshop."

"Whatever." After a moment she added, "It was nice of you guys to give up the bedrooms. I really didn't know you were stuck out here."

Gabe leaned a hip on the table. "I kind of like it—the seclusion. I could've bunked in the family room, but this offers more privacy."

Dena must have changed clothes after her swim. She now wore a snug moss-green brocade vest that might have actually looked prim if there'd been anything under it, and a very short, hip-hugging, white skirt belted with a clear plastic, daisy-studded belt that matched her shoes. Her navel peeked out the notched bottom of the vest, but it was her legs that grabbed his attention and held it, those gorgeous smooth, suntanned legs that went on and on. And on and on and on.

She glanced at the work spread out on the table. "Is this what you went back for this morning?"

"Yep."

"You forgot to bring it out on Saturday?" She looked skeptical.

A better lie came to him. "Something urgent came up. I got word about it yesterday, so I had to go back for the paperwork."

"They couldn't courier it out here?"

I had to pick up clothes, too. "They never would've sent everything I needed, and I'd have lost even more time."

Dena strolled around the room, perusing the contents of Ham's workshop, those silly, sexy shoes clicking on the wooden floor. "You're a partner now, Gabe. High muck-a-muck. You have to learn to delegate."

"Speaking of which—who's minding the store at Xanadu? The summer months must be your busy season."

"I have managers at all my locations—good people—and an assistant who's been with me practically from the beginning. I'm in touch every day by phone and fax, and it's not like I'm on the other side of the world. All the resorts are in or close to the New York metropolitan area. I can get to any of them within a couple of hours."

"Have you thought of expanding out of the region?"

For some reason, this comment drew a frosty stare. "I have no desire to discuss my business plans with you."

Gabe scowled. "Just a friendly question."

She regarded him with disdain. "Andrea already treated me to the hard sell, and I'll tell you what I told her. It's not happening. I'm happy with Gilliam, Shapiro."

Oh hell. "Dena, I wasn't trying to... Do you think I'd make a play for your business after not seeing you for fifteen years, after what happened between us? Come on."

Dena stood under a skylight; the brilliant sunshine turned her hair to gleaming platinum. She crossed her arms under her full breasts, nudging even more cleavage into the vest's V-neckline. "Please, Gabe. I know you and Andrea discussed it. Don't treat me like a fool."

A sound rumbled up his throat, something between a sigh and a growl. "Yes, we discussed it, because Andrea was insistent on approaching you. She has tunnel vision when it comes to developing new business for the firm. I told her it was... inappropriate for either one of us to go after you. I assumed that would be the end of it."

Dena studied him as if gauging his sincerity.

"I'm genuinely sorry," Gabe said. "You shouldn't have had to put up with that." Recalling how artfully she'd handled Andrea yesterday, and Frank and Dave on Saturday, he added, "Can I assume you made her sorry she asked?"

A reluctant smile tugged at her mouth. "I think it's safe to say she's scratched Xanadu off her list of prospective clients."

Gabe bit his lower lip, stifling his mirth. He shouldn't take satisfaction in his partner's defeat. After all, his principal mandate at Moreau Pittman was to bring in new business. Against his will, his imagination drew a picture of Dena in all her self-righteous glory cutting Andrea down to size. The chuckle burst from him, and he said, "I wish I could've witnessed that."

She met his gaze, and in that instant they seemed to be on the same wavelength. *It's still there*, he thought. The bond they'd shared—once robust, nourished by their love and trust, now buried under the weight of his betrayal and their years apart. Withered from neglect, but not dead.

Dena blinked and it was gone, like a phone connection cut off. "Ham sent me for some more hickory wood." She looked around. "He said there was a storage room through here?"

"This way." Gabe crossed to the windowless wall and opened the door. As he entered the small, dark space and groped for a light switch, he sensed Dena behind him, detected the heat of her body. The hickory smoke hadn't penetrated here, and Gabe's nostrils flared, drinking in the provocative scent that was hers alone.

"I think I see a pull-cord," she said, jostling against him in the close confines of the storage room.

Gabe's breath snagged as she wriggled past him. How many times had he lain awake, recalling the feel of Dena pressing her lush body against him in the back seat of his Camaro? It had the same effect on him now as it had had then. He discreetly shifted away, swearing silently, willing his erection to subside.

Dena pulled a chain hanging from the ceiling, revealing a bare bulb and filling the little room with harsh light. Perhaps it was his imagination, but her color looked a little high, and she avoided his eyes. Was it possible she'd experienced a few sleepless nights herself?

"Hickory...hickory...hickory..." she chanted, peering at the contents of the plank shelves perched on metal brackets lining both long walls. "Hickory dickory dock." A wide array of household items occupied the shelves, from bags of rock salt to cases of soda to a little-used milk-glass punch bowl set.

"Here it is." Gabe lifted a yellow plastic bucket filled with small chunks of wood. "I can only assume this is hickory."

"Great." Dena moved to take the bucket from

him, but he carried it himself, gesturing for her to precede him out of the storage room.

"I'd better get this to Ham," Dena said. "It's got to soak before he can—"

"Wait a second," Gabe said, as his heartbeat revved up a notch. He set the bucket on the floor and crossed to his suitcase, where he'd deposited a small paper sack. "I stopped at this little antiques place on the way out here and, well...when I saw this, I thought of you." He handed her the bag and she accepted it gingerly. He'd seen people contemplate containers of live bait with more enthusiasm.

"You bought me something?"

"Open it." He crossed his arms, then immediately uncrossed them and leaned a sweaty palm on the worktable. "It's nothing. Just a little...it's really nothing."

"Oh!" Her face lit in a delighted smile as she pulled the tiny porcelain figurine from the bag. "It's a pug! A black one!"

Black pugs—the kind Dena raised—were much less common than brown. "I don't suppose you still have Mildred and Horace. They'd be, what? A hundred fifty in dog years by now?"

Dena turned the figurine around, admiring it from all angles. "Those two rascals are long gone, but I kept one of their descendants, Hermione. She's pregnant, and living it up this week at the Xanadu resort in Garden City. This looks just like her!"

Gabe breathed a relieved sigh. "I'm glad you like it."

Dena's smile faded. Resignedly she tucked the

pug back in the sack, crimped the top closed and held it out to him.

An oppressive weight pulled at Gabe's insides. "Dena, I bought it for you."

"I can't accept this, Gabe."

"It doesn't mean anything. I mean..." He scrubbed at the back of his neck. "It's just a stupid little statue. Take it."

"I just can't...I won't accept anything from you, Gabe, not even this." She thrust it toward him more forcefully. "I'm sorry."

Woodenly he took the bag from her and set it on the table. "No, I'm sorry. I never intended to put you on the spot."

She looked away, hugging herself, and Gabe saw her chin wobble.

"Dena, love, don't..." He found himself enfolding her in his arms, a reflexive gesture devoid of guile. She stiffened for an instant, then relaxed and let him hold her.

Gabe pressed her head to his shoulder, his fingers sliding over her scalp. He felt every shuddering breath as she fought to contain the tears.

"Dena..." he whispered, holding her tighter. She'd grown into a strong, independent woman. But even the strongest people needed someone to lean on once in a while, needed someone *else* to be strong for a change. Gabe wondered how long it had been since Dena had had someone to lean on. "Go ahead, cry if you want."

She shook her head.

"It's just us," he murmured, stroking the fragrant silk of her hair, nuzzling it. "No one else will see."

Her watery voice was so quiet he almost didn't

hear it. "I don't know why I feel like crying. It's so stupid. There's no reason for it."

He rubbed her back in slow circles. "How about because I'm a clueless oaf who only manages to make things worse? There's a reason for you."

"You didn't... It's not..." She let out a long, shaky sigh. "It's complicated. The whole thing's so *damn* complicated."

That was good news, as far as Gabe was concerned. "Complicated" meant she had conflicting emotions regarding him. It wasn't much, but he'd take it.

Still holding her close, Gabe pressed a lingering kiss to her hair. He tipped her face up. Her cheeks were dry, but her eyes glistened. The pupils were pinpoints in the sunlight slanting from overhead, the surrounding irises startlingly green.

"I'm going to kiss you," he whispered, and felt her breathing quicken, watched those conflicting emotions chase one another across her face.

As he lowered his head she started to say something, but then his mouth touched hers and he inhaled her soft gasp. He'd never forgotten this, he realized, as he tangled his fingers in her hair. He'd never forgotten the shape of her mouth against his, the exquisite softness of her lips, the intoxicating taste of her.

The kiss was tender, cherishing. Gabe struggled with his rampant need, wanting to give more than he took. Dena whimpered, pushing at his chest even as her mouth shifted under his, plucking at his lips. His arms clamped tightly around her. He knew she felt his arousal, stiff as a post against her belly. He knew and he didn't care.

Gabe parted her mouth with his and stroked her with the tip of his tongue. She trembled and pressed closer, her hands sliding to his shoulders, clutching at him. He tasted her deeply, penetrating and receding in an unmistakable rhythm. Her tongue slid against his, matching the cadence. He groaned deep in his throat, his exhilaration tempered by the knowledge that she would chastise herself later, for responding to him.

Gabe couldn't say who pulled away first. Breathless, he rested his forehead on Dena's, already formulating a rebuttal to her inevitable self-recriminations. His gut twisted when he heard her weeping.

"Oh, love..." Gently he lifted her face to his, only to be struck dumb by the merriment he saw there. It wasn't crying he'd heard, but giddy laughter!

"That's the other effect I have on women," he said. "If I had one of those frail male egos you hear so much about, I might start getting my feelings hurt right about now."

Dena stepped away from him as her giggles died down. "You're still the best kisser I've ever known."

Gabe responded with a nonchalant little smile that said, *No surprise there*, while inside he was grinning like the village idiot. "I see," he said. "Your hilarity makes perfect sense now."

"Oh, stop," she said. "I don't know why I'm laughing any more than I know why I felt like crying. A release of tension—I guess that's all it is." Her gaze flicked to the small sack sitting on the table.

Gabe shoved his hands in the pockets of his

denim shorts and kept his distance, wary of jeopardizing the fragile accord he sensed developing between them. "I was afraid you'd be upset."

"By a kiss?"

"Well…"

"I know I said you were the best, Gabe, but let's face it." She shrugged. "It's still just a kiss."

"'A kiss is still a kiss,'" he sang, hand to chest, "'a sigh is still a sigh…'"

"And Ham is still waiting for this hickory," she said, lifting the bucket. "I'm surprised he hasn't started hollering for it yet." She frowned. "You don't suppose he just forgot about it? His memory used to be so sharp. But lately…"

Privately, Gabe thought their old friend's memory lapses were suspiciously well timed, but he chose not to share the observation. Taking the bucket from her, he started toward the door to the breezeway. "As long as he remembers how to make that killer brisket of his, he can forget his own name, for all I care. If you ask me nicely, I'll help you shuck all that corn we bought at the farm stand."

"*You'll* help *me*? Who was it who insisted on buying two dozen ears?" She held the door open for him.

"Only because I remembered it's your favorite vegetable."

"But *two dozen ears*? It may be my favorite vegetable, Gabe, but let's face it—"

"I know, I know." He grinned. "It's still just corn."

6

"WHO ARE THE METS playing tonight?" Frank asked from the back seat as Dena pulled her dark blue Lincoln Navigator up the long asphalt driveway and parked next to Ham's house.

"The Atlanta Braves," Scott said, opening the front passenger door and hopping out. "Should be a great game. When are we leaving for Shea?"

"No later than four-thirty," Rhonda answered. "It's a long drive to Queens, and who knows what parking will be like." Opening the back door, she struggled to descend the vehicle's high step while clutching her denim skirt around her knees.

Frank grunted as he let himself out the other side. "Don't you know these SUVs are practically passé?" he asked Dena. "I'm surprised you don't drive some kinda sports car. A 'Vette maybe."

Dena sprang out of the vehicle and slammed the door. "I'm always transporting dogs. This thing fits the bill."

Ham and Reba had taken their own car on this morning's excursion, and they weren't back yet. Only Gabe and Andrea had remained at the house, working together in his room on some legal case. Against her will, the image of Gabe's cot sprang to mind, the bedding in disarray.

No! she commanded herself. *Don't even go there.*

As far as she was concerned, Andrea was welcome to him.

Scott's hand on her back rousted the dark thoughts. "So who do you like, the Mets or the Yankees?" he asked. Every New Yorker had a preference.

"Oh, definitely the Mets. Could you see me rooting for any team that wears pinstripes?"

There was that yummy, dark-eyed smile again. She'd seen a lot of that this morning as they'd wandered the house and grounds of Sagamore Hill, Theodore Roosevelt's home in Cove Neck, where Scott had turned ventriloquist and put hilarious words in the mouths of the many stuffed trophy heads adorning the walls. They'd also visited Old Bethpage Village, a collection of nineteenth-century buildings that offered a glimpse into the past, complete with a blacksmith, hatter, general store and farm animals.

Dena had done a lot of driving and a lot of walking. She was tired, but it was nothing that a swim and a mug or two of Reba's strong coffee wouldn't cure.

"I'd better ride in your car tonight," Scott said, as he accompanied her into the house. "Without my expert navigational skills, we might end up in Pennsylvania."

"I never claimed to have a sense of direction."

Dena had taken a lot of ribbing for that particular failing. If Scott hadn't been sitting next to her earlier, with one eye on the map and the other on road signs, she might indeed have ended up in Pennsylvania.

During their outing she'd learned how Scott had

come to be a Presbyterian minister. Academically, he'd been in the top ten percent of their high-school class, but instead of attending college, he'd become a professional ballplayer, eventually signing with the Rochester Red Wings, the triple-A farm team for the Baltimore Orioles. After his wife's death, his initial self-pity had gradually evolved into a more constructive introspection, leading him to his true calling. He'd attended Columbia University, followed by Princeton Seminary, and had ultimately become the pastor of a small congregation in Ohio.

Dena couldn't help wonder, as she watched Scott descend the basement steps to the fifties-style rec room he referred to as Knotty Pine Estates, whether his offer to ride shotgun was motivated purely by a desire to keep her from getting lost.

Did she want it to be?

"Don't go there either," she grumbled to herself as she made her way upstairs to her room. It was confusing enough just seeing Gabe again, when she'd long ago archived that youthful chapter of her life under "Excruciating Learning Experiences." Romantic speculation involving Reverend Yummy was more than she could deal with at the moment.

Dena thought back to last night as she changed into a one-shoulder leopard-print swimsuit complete with ragged cavewoman fringe, which she'd bought because it reminded her of Raquel Welch in *One Million Years B.C.* The reunion crowd—forty or so including spouses—had attended a local theater production of a play written by a Long Island playwright and starring a well-known movie actor. Gabe had none-too-subtly maneuvered to sit next to her in the theater, and had stayed close to her at the dance club where the more energetic members of the group had congregated later.

She hadn't danced with Gabe since high school, and had been unprepared for the rush of carnal awareness that had stormed her senses like a fever. Recalling the way he'd looked at her, the smoky potency of his gaze, she suspected he'd felt it too.

Back when they'd been dating she'd allowed her emotions free rein, delighting in their mutual attraction, in the exquisite anticipation of the act that would embody their love and seal their commitment. She recalled her innocent fascination with the physical aspect of their relationship, the petting and fondling, the bottomless kisses and constant, bone-deep craving.

Now, fifteen years after it had all fallen apart, she grappled with the resurgence of that mutual attraction, recognizing it for the rudimentary chemical reaction it was. Hormones. Pheromones. The same thing that used to happen between Mildred and Horace.

Yeah, right.

It was turning into a long week.

Dena slipped on her orange satin robe and pink glitter mules, grabbed a towel from the bathroom and headed downstairs.

She was about to push open the screen door when Gabe's voice came to her from across the breezeway separating the workshop from the house. One of the workshop's open windows was directly across from the door she stood behind. She saw him cross the room, his stride lazy, unhurried. He was talking to someone.

"...wish I could be there. Give Aunt Caroline my best."

He disappeared, and reappeared walking in the other direction. Dena now saw he held a cordless phone to his ear. He stopped by the worktable and idly flipped through a file as he conversed.

"Well, sometimes plans change at the last minute, Mother. It wouldn't hurt you to be more flexible."

An image of Cynthia Moreau popped into Dena's head, the epitome of understated elegance with her Chanel suits and carefully tinted honey-blond hair and brittle plastic smile. *And what colleges are you applying to, dear...? A dog groomer? Well, I suppose you can always change your mind later.*

"No, I won't be back until Saturday," Gabe was saying. "That's right, the whole week. We're staying with Ham Conklin, me and Andrea and some others."

He looked up then, straight out the window, and Dena shrank back into the shadowed hallway, though she knew he couldn't see her.

"No one special," he said, "just a few people I went to school with." He slapped the file closed and parked his hip on the edge of the table.

No one special.

Silently she turned from the door and, in a spineless move worthy of the old Dena, retreated down the hallway.

FROM HER FIELD-LEVEL BOX SEAT five rows behind first base, Dena watched John Franco pitch a high fast ball to the Braves batter, who fouled it off about ten rows behind her. Bedlam ensued as fans vaulted over seats in a mad scramble for the ball.

Next to her, Gabe was grinning. "I haven't been to a game in years. Didn't realize how much I missed it."

"My friend Margaret and I come here to see the Mets play at least three or four times each season," Dena said. "She's in love with Mike Piazza."

Dena pitied Gabe the grueling work schedule that kept him from the simple pleasures of a ball game: The crack of the bat, the din of the crowd surging to their feet to cheer in a home run, the blare of the sound system trumpeting our boys to victory. *Da-da-da-DUM-da-DUM…CHARGE!!!* The mingled perfumes of cold beer and hot frankfurters. The sticky patina of spilled soda underfoot. The unrivaled ambrosia of stadium peanuts.

Heaven.

It was the top of the eighth and the Mets were leading three to one. The floodlights ringing the top of the stadium were on, illuminating the field, while overhead the sky was dark and overcast. A sudden breeze blew in, cool and moist and smelling of rain. Dena prayed it would hold off for another inning and a half.

Their group occupied several rows. Dena sat on the aisle. Just like last night at the theater, Gabe had lost no time snagging the seat next to hers.

"So tell me," she asked, as the batter hit the ball into shallow left field for a base hit. "Even with the incredible workload, the ungodly hours, missing all those Mets games and who knows what else—are you happy?"

"Yes." He didn't hesitate. ' I'm doing what I've always wanted to do."

"And doing it very well, by all appearances. So that's it, then. You've executed your master plan. You've got the corner office, the centerfold condo. Life's complete."

He wore a wry grin. "Do I detect a trace of sarcasm?"

"No, you detect a whole big heaping shovelful of it. But hey..." She shrugged. "Different strokes for different folks. I bet you could never imagine playing innkeeper to dogs and cats, either."

"When I was younger I'd have dismissed something like that out of hand as flaky in the extreme."

"Not to put too fine a point on it, but my flaky business is hauling in the green stuff by the bucketload."

Gabe raised his hand. "I said that's what I would've thought back then. Youthful tunnel vision." He met her gaze directly. "I'm not the same stupid kid."

Studying his earnest face under the cool stadium lights, Dena knew he wasn't just talking about business. They stared at each other even when the skies opened like a tipped bucket, dumping rain on their heads, even when everyone around them leaped out of their seats to wait out the storm in the enclosed perimeter of the stadium.

Dena finally moved to rise. Gabe stopped her with a hand on her arm. He produced the umbrella she'd razzed him for bringing along—"there's only a thirty percent chance of rain, Gabe!"—and opened it over their heads. It was enormous, a big, black executive model, covering them both with room to spare.

"A family of six could live under here," Dena said, as rain battered the surrounding orange plastic seats and drummed on the taut nylon fabric overhead. The great bowl of the stadium, packed to capacity two minutes earlier, now appeared deserted, save for a cluster of fans huddled under the overhang circling the top. The floodlights mounted there turned the downpour into a glittering curtain. The grounds crew were lined up behind an enormous cylinder, unrolling a blue tarpaulin over the infield.

Gabe's eyes glowed like polished amber in the murky half-light of their domelike shelter. Dena pushed her wet hair off her face and rubbed her arms, rough with gooseflesh. Gabe transferred the umbrella to his other hand and put his arm around her. She leaned into his heat, knowing she should get up and join the others, but lacking the will to do so.

"It's funny," she murmured, snuggled against his shoulder but not looking at him, "you saying you're not the same stupid kid. I never thought of you as stupid back then. I adored you. To me you were...perfect. You were all I wanted, all I could ever imagine wanting."

"I guess on some level I knew that," he said after a moment. "You put me up on a pedestal, and it never occurred to me that there's only one place to go from there."

Straight down. But he'd toppled himself, Dena silently argued. She might have been young and naive and hopelessly besotted, but his actions were his own doing. He couldn't claim she'd driven him into the arms of another.

Dena felt Gabe turn his head, felt his warm, humid breath on her face. He was looking at her. "I've thought about it a lot over the years," he said. "About what led up to…"

A gentle sigh wafted over her. The hand draped over her shoulder shifted and he stroked her bare upper arm. Outside the haven of their umbrella, the downpour continued unabated. The grounds crew had finished their work; the infield was now one giant blue patch.

"I had blinders on, too, in a way." He seemed to choose his words with care. "My world back then was strictly circumscribed. I mean, I went to public school, I played basketball, I did the drama club and all that, but that was only part of who I was. And not the biggest part."

"You mean you didn't have to work a paper route to buy shoes? I kind of knew that already, Gabe."

"What I mean is, the way I was brought up—it was all I knew, all I was really comfortable with. My parents raised me to think the world revolved around me. I was the only son, crown prince of the family empire. We only associated with people like us, people who lived the way we did, who'd gone to the same schools, joined the same clubs."

Dena said, "So I was what? Your walk on the sleazy side?"

She tried to pull away, but Gabe wouldn't let her. His face a hairbreadth from hers, his golden eyes burning into her, he said, "No. I was sheltered and shallow—and too damn full of myself to admit it or even recognize it. If I failed to appreciate you—your strengths, your potential—it was because I had no frame of reference. I couldn't compartmentalize you. You didn't come with a label."

"Such as 'Debutante Daughter of Daddy's Law Partner.'"

"This has nothing to do with her," he said sharply. "It has nothing to do with what happened. Well, it does," he amended, "but I won't get into that. Not until you're ready."

"I've said it before. We never really knew each other." Dena stared out at the rain, now dwindling to a light shower. "I practically deified you. And as far as you were concerned, I was this loose cannon you could never quite figure out."

Despite everything, she grinned. Poor Gabe. What courage it must have taken for the crown prince to bring Elly May Clampett home to meet the king and queen.

"I've become a bit more broad-minded since then," he said dryly. "I've had to. Losing you may have been my most painful learning experience, but it was by no means my last."

I'm not the same stupid kid. A telling comment, considering how confident Gabe had always acted in high school. It had been one of the things that had initially attracted her to him. The man he'd become had depths to him the boy could never have foreseen or appreciated. He didn't pretend to have an answer for everything.

"Dena."

She looked at him, and in his eyes she read his stark sincerity.

"I don't believe that," he said, "that we never

knew each other—and I don't think you believe it either. There was always something there—something very special."

Then why did you throw it away? she wanted to ask, but she didn't. Clearly he'd done a lot of soul-searching, but she wasn't ready to hear more.

Perhaps Gabe sensed that, because he didn't try to pursue it. Rising, he closed the umbrella and shook it out, and only then did Dena notice it had stopped raining. Fans were drifting back into the stadium, wiping down the seats with whatever was handy. On the infield the grounds crew began the laborious task of rerolling the tarp.

Dena rose, too, and stretched. Gabe glanced up the aisle. Rhonda was returning to her seat. Ever efficient, she carried a stack of rest-room paper towels to dry the seats. Frank followed close behind, his own arms laden with nachos, caramel corn and beer.

Gabe wasted no time. "Dena, you don't want to go on that garden tour tomorrow. Don't lie to me."

She didn't even try. To her, flowers and gardening were a major yawn. "What did you have in mind?"

His gaze shot to Rhonda "the Mouth" Peterson, fast approaching but still out of earshot. "Come with me to the beach. Just the two of us. We'll bum around for the day."

Just the thought of it brought such pure, incandescent bliss to Gabe's face that Dena had to laugh. When was the last time he'd lazed around on a beach? She'd bet her prettiest pug he spent nearly every weekend working. Still, she had to point out, "They're relying on us to drive."

"They don't need us to chauffeur them around. Ham can drive a couple of them, and one of the locals can swing by and pick up the rest. Shouldn't be too hard to line up a ride—close to twenty people are going on that garden tour."

"Well..."

Rhonda was three rows away, her progress hampered by her self-imposed role as distributor of the paper towels.

Gabe sidled closer to Dena and whispered, "Tell them you're sick—allergic to the flowers, there you go. I'll claim I have transmission trouble and have to take the car in. As soon as they're gone—" his arm skated straight out "—we blow the joint."

A date? With Gabe? What was she thinking?

He said, "It's not a date, if that's what you're thinking. Say yes. Nod your head. Send up a smoke signal. Anything."

Dena thought of all those weekends Gabe spent poring over law books and depositions and who knew what all, when he should have been adding to his seashell collection. She said, "I'll pack the sunscreen."

7

FROM HER BEDROOM WINDOW Dena watched Gil Reyes's station wagon pull out of the driveway, with Rhonda and Frank inside. She figured Scott and Andrea must have gotten a ride earlier with Ham. The day was pleasantly warm but not blistering, the vivid blue sky studded with puffy cumulus clouds. The perfect day for a garden tour.

Or the beach.

She smiled, thoroughly enjoying the naughty pleasure of playing hooky. *All it would take is one whiff of those flowers*, she'd told Rhonda last night, *and my allergies would level me like a freight train. I could stop breathing!*

Rhonda's nose had already been out of joint due to Gabe's sudden transmission trouble. This double whammy was wreaking havoc with her careful planning. Without skipping a beat, Ham had cheerfully picked up the phone and called Gil Reyes, who lived in the next town, to help with transportation.

Ham's sanguine attitude struck Dena as odd, considering how anxious he'd been to have both her and Gabe available for these kinds of chores. Perhaps mood swings were another manifestation of the aging process, Dena thought as she moved away from the window and opened a dresser dra ver.

Which swimsuit to wear? She'd brought an even dozen. One by one she lifted them, idly speculating on Gabe's reaction to each. When she realized what she was doing she chided herself and grabbed one at random. After a moment's hesitation she shoved the simple black-and-white maillot back in the drawer and pulled out her prettiest, sexiest suit.

Well, hell, she'd brought it not even knowing Gabe would be here this week. Why *shouldn't* she wear it?

Dena quickly stripped off her short red sundress and stepped into the slinky navy one-piece. Sheer navy mesh fabric extended above the deeply plunging neckline, giving it the appearance of lingerie. The same mesh filled a diamond-shaped cutout on the midriff. The suit dipped to the waist in back and was cut high on the thighs, making her legs look even longer. Slipping her feet into towering white platform sandals, she grabbed her sunscreen, slung an oversize white T-shirt over her arm and headed downstairs to find Gabe.

The first floor was deserted, so she crossed the breezeway to the workshop, only to discover it was empty as well. Could he be at the pool? Crossing to the window, she scanned the backyard. Nothing. On her way to the door she spied a yellow legal pad on the worktable. A note had been scrawled on it.

Dena,
Something came up at work. Andrea and I had to go to the office. I'll call you later.

G

G? she fumed, ripping the page off the pad and wadding it up. *The man can't even take the trouble to sign his name?*

He hadn't had the common decency to knock on her door and tell her in person. If he had, she might have decided to go on that stupid garden tour after all. What was she supposed to do with herself all day? Sit around waiting for His Highness to call?

No one special, he'd told his mother when she'd asked who was staying at Ham's. Which made sense, when you thought about it. This was certainly the way you treated no one special.

Dena stalked out of the workshop and into the house, slamming doors and stomping her platform shoes all over the bare wood floors. So she was acting infantile. So what? No one was around to witness her performance, and it made her feel better.

No it didn't. She didn't know who she was more angry with, Gabe for standing her up, or herself for allowing it to happen. In the huge country kitchen she tossed her shirt and sunscreen on the counter and threw open the refrigerator, scavenging for breakfast leftovers. She was starved, having sequestered herself in her room that morning, loath to endure the inevitable, protracted discussion of her "allergies." She had no desire to compound her lie or listen to well-meaning advice on the latest nondrowsy medication.

Particularly since she was, as far as she knew, allergic to absolutely nothing.

There it was, on the bottom shelf, a platter of leftover pancakes and sausage. All she had to do was nuke it in the microwave. She grabbed the platter, turned around, and nearly dropped it as a scream barreled up her throat.

"Don't sneak up on people like that!" she cried, pressing a hand to her thumping heart.

Scott stood near the entrance to the basement, scratching his bare chest, wearing nothing but a pair of white boxer shorts embellished with pictures of exploding firecrackers. His thick salt-and-pepper hair was sleep-rumpled. "I thought everyone was gone. Till I heard the racket up here."

"Oh. I was, uh…I thought I was alone."

He sauntered into the kitchen, eyeing the pancakes and sausage. "Enough for two?" He lifted the carafe from the coffeemaker and poured the dregs into two stoneware mugs, causing the knotted-rope tattoo circling his right biceps to stretch.

"More than enough. I take it you skipped breakfast, too?" Dena peeled the plastic wrap off the food. Scott opened the door of the microwave, and she slid the platter inside.

"Slept in," he said. "I don't know a pansy from a chrysanthemum, and that's the way I intend to keep it. So who are you angry at?"

"Who says I'm angry? How the hell do you turn this thing on?" she asked, stabbing blindly at the microwave keypad.

He shooed her hands away, studied the keypad for three seconds and pushed two buttons. The machine started humming. "Is it Gabe?"

As Dena opened her mouth to deny it, Scott crossed his arms and gravely intoned, "I'm a man of the cloth. You can't fib to me."

She eyed the good reverend up and down. "Well, you'll excuse me if that little fact kind of slipped my mind for a moment. Perhaps if you wore your clerical collar with that getup, it might help."

He glanced down at the firecracker undies. "The church secretary gave them to me for my birthday."

"Which is—let me guess—the Fourth of July." She hauled the jug of maple syrup out of the fridge.

"A Yankee Doodle dandy, that's me. Speaking of intriguing getups..." He stared pointedly at Dena's sexy swimsuit.

"I was...going to go for a swim."

"*Were* going to go for a swim? No more?"

"I don't know what I'm going to do," she snapped. "I have the whole damn day to figure it out."

The microwave beeped and she yanked hard on the door handle, with no success. Scott reached over and pushed the button marked Open Door.

"You know, you're really getting on my nerves," she said, as he set the platter on a corner of the work island in the middle of the kitchen and pulled knives and forks out of a drawer.

"You're projecting your anger on me because Gabe stood you up." He started eating right off the platter.

"Who said Gabe stood me up?"

Mouth full, he said, "I counsel people all the time. I'm a trained professional." He wagged his fork at her. "Kids, don't try this at home."

"He had to go back to the city." She hacked at a stack of pancakes and skewered a big wad on her fork. "With Andrea. If his work is so damn important, why is he even staying out here all week?"

"That sounds like a good question to ask him."

"Forget it. I don't even want to talk to him. It was

a mistake to even—" She broke off with something between a growl and a screech, bayonetting a sausage link with far more zeal than the task required.

"Looks like he got that transmission fixed pretty fast," Scott said, deadpan.

The look she gave him said she could do without the pithy observations.

He asked, "So do you think he has a thing going with Andrea?"

"I don't know. Probably. It makes no difference to me." She sawed the sausage into bite-size pieces.

"Because I don't really know the guy," he said, "but I know the *look*, if you know what I mean."

"I don't. No."

"The look when a guy's interested. And he doesn't have it. With Andrea."

"That doesn't mean anything. They've known each other for years. Hell, they've known each other forever. Their mothers shared a *baby shower*, of all things! They were born less than a month apart. Their families have had them unofficially engaged since they were spitting up pablum."

"But it didn't take."

"What?"

"They never got married. What do you think they're waiting for? Hey, leave some sausage for me."

Dena attacked the last link. "Well, why should he buy the cow when he's getting the milk for free? Isn't that the expression? Maybe they're just waiting till they're ready to have kids. I don't know. Although he did say…"

"What?"

"Well, he said he hadn't met the right woman— when I asked why he wasn't married."

"Do you believe that?"

She hesitated. "Why shouldn't I?"

Scott didn't answer. He scraped up the last of the pancakes and laid down his fork. "I found the right woman," he said at last, and Dena knew he was referring to Annie Goode, his high-school sweetheart who'd died within two years of their wedding. "That's the good news. The bad news is, she's gone and I can never get her back."

"Scott." Dena's eyes stung. She remembered how close he and Annie had been in high school. "Someday you'll meet someone else who's right for you."

"Maybe." He smiled gently. "Maybe not. When Annie was taken from me, I was angry. Angry at her for leaving me, angry at God for letting it happen, angry at myself for not somehow preventing it. You know, the 'if only' game. If only I'd made her go to the doctor sooner, if only I'd paid more attention to her headaches...

"It took me a long time to come to terms with her death, and with my faith. I think that experience has helped me counsel couples who are having problems. As bad as those problems sometimes are, I'd give anything to be in their shoes. They still have a chance to be together."

Dena couldn't look at him. She knew he was talking about her and Gabe, she knew she should tell him to keep his unsolicited advice to himself, but somehow the words wouldn't come.

How could everything have gotten so complicated in four short days?

Dena felt his hand on her arm, a fleeting touch.

Scott carried the platter and flatware to the dishwasher. When he turned back to her he said, "I'll meet you down here in fifteen minutes. Is your map still in the car?"

"Yeah, but...where are we going?"

He smiled. "It's a surprise."

"What should I wear?"

"Well, I'm tempted to say, come as you are...." His appreciative gaze lingered on the sheer parts of her suit. "But shorts and a T-shirt should do it. Oh, and sneakers."

"Sneakers? Ugh."

"Do you own a pair?"

"Yes, I *own* a pair," she replied, indignant.

"'Cause I was going to offer to lend you some. Looks like we wear about the same size."

"One more crack about my big feet and I don't go anywhere with you. And *I'm* the one with the car."

Scott pointed imperiously toward the staircase. "Fifteen minutes."

8

WHEN GABE FINALLY located Dena, she was standing with her back to him, staring at a barrel-chested suit of plate armor featuring elaborate scrollwork and a wicked-looking codpiece of equine proportions.

She wore a form-fitting coral-colored silk dress with iridescent threads running through it. The dress seemed to comprise two layers, sheer chiffon over an opaque underslip. Thin spaghetti straps exposed shoulders that looked more sun-kissed than they had yesterday. Had she gone to the beach without him? Looking past the flowing calf-length skirt, Gabe saw spike-heeled metallic sandals in a pewter tone.

He'd just driven uptown from his office on Wall Street, still dressed in khaki shorts and a black T-shirt, the clothes he'd thrown on that morning in his haste. Not exactly suitable attire for a private reception at the Metropolitan Museum of Art followed by dinner at the Harvard Club, but he'd had to see Dena.

He wondered if it meant anything that he'd found her perusing the museum's extensive armaments collection. Gil and Cookie Reyes strolled nearby, chatting softly. Gabe waited until they'd disappeared into the next gallery, then he silently walked up behind Dena.

She became very still, as if she possessed some sort of internal warning system alerting her to his presence.

He asked, "What do you think that guy did when he had an itch?"

Dena cocked her head, studying the suit of armor. "I think he probably wished they'd hurry up and invent Kevlar."

She turned to face him, outwardly cordial, but Gabe wasn't fooled. Her gaze held no warmth.

"You're angry," he said. "I left you a note."

"Yes, you did," she agreed, too calm. "Thank you."

Ham and Reba entered the room, and Gabe lowered his voice. "I tried to call you. Five times. There was no answer."

"I wasn't there." Dena greeted Ham and Reba, prompting them to amble over. She'd done it purely to vex Gabe, he was sure.

Ham consulted the pocket watch tucked into his baggy white painter's paints, which he'd paired with a mold-green bowling shirt with his name stitched onto it. Well, at least Gabe had competition for most inappropriately dressed. Reba was, as usual, impeccably turned out in a pale taupe suit with matching spectator pumps. Not a blue hair out of place.

"We should start heading out to the street," Ham said. "It'll take eight or nine cabs to get us all down to the Harvard Club."

"I don't know, Ham," Gabe teased, as the two couples made their way through galleries toward the front of the museum. "I'm kind of afraid to let you into that bastion of stodginess. Don't know what mischief you might get up to. They could end up revoking my membership."

Ham said, "I was there once. When FDR was in office. All I remember is dark paneling and cigar smoke and old farts dozing in leather club chairs with the *Wall Street Journal* spread out on their laps."

Gabe slapped him on the back. "Well, prepare yourself for a time warp, my friend. It's the same place you remember."

Dena said, "Except that nowadays, some of that cigar smoke is being blown by women."

"And once in a while you actually see an old fart in there wearing a bowling shirt and painter's pants," Reba added, with an impish smile.

"Plenty of progress for six decades, wouldn't you say?" Ham asked dryly.

Evening traffic was thick on Fifth Avenue. About a dozen of their fellow reunion-goers were clustered outside the museum, hailing cabs, so the foursome walked a block downtown and got a taxi within half a minute, with help from Ham's earsplitting whistle. Gabe took the front passenger seat. Dena sat in the back between Ham and Reba.

Reba turned to Dena. "I understand you had quite an adventure today."

"What did you do?" Ham asked.

"Scott took me whale-watching out of Montauk Point," Dena said, in a tone of voice bordering on rapturous.

So, Gabe thought sourly. Now he knew why she hadn't answered the phone.

Had *anyone* gone on that garden tour?

"Oh, that sounds lovely!" Reba said. "I've always wanted to do that. Did you see any whales?"

"We sure did. A couple of finbacks, these great gray beasts as long as the boat. They didn't do much, just kind of floated there, sizing us up, I guess. But there were also these little guys—well, little for whales. Minkes, they're called, and they're really spirited, frolicking around in the water. I could have watched them forever."

How could a day at the beach compete with whale-watching? Gabe thought—uncharitably, he knew. He was, after all, the one who'd left her in the lurch. He should be glad she'd salvaged the day and had such a great time.

With Scott.

"I'd never seen whales in the wild before," Dena gushed. "It was incredible! And we saw sharks—basking sharks, they're called. They're about as big as the minkes and they just kind of move slowly along the surface of the water...."

"Basking in the sun?" Gabe said.

"Well, that's what it looks like, but they're really feeding, straining plankton. And we saw these huge, ugly sunfish, too. And birds—seagulls, of course, but also gannets and petrels, birds you really only see out on the ocean. The boat's a research vessel that doubles as a whale-watching boat."

"Well, it sounds like you and Scott had a very special day," Reba said. "Such a sweet boy. So sad about his wife. Wouldn't it be wonderful if he found some nice girl and settled down?"

It sounded to Gabe as if the "sweet boy" was working on it.

The taxi let them off on Forty-fourth Street in front of the Harvard Club, with its burgundy-colored awning and marble steps leading to the foyer. Gabe grasped Dena's arm, detaining her on the sidewalk as the others entered the building. The tide of pedestrians flowed around them with barely a ripple.

"Listen," he said, "I didn't want to break our date today, but sometimes things happen."

"I thought it wasn't a date."

He sighed in exasperation. "You *are* angry. Just hear me out for a second."

"I really don't feel like getting into this out here on the sidewalk."

He released her arm. "Correction. You really don't feel like getting into it, period. You have no use for explanations, isn't that right? You never did."

"What's the point of—"

"As far as you're concerned, you've been wronged, and nothing can excuse it." *Déjà vu.*

"You're very good at twisting things around," she said. "Do you do that in the courtroom, too? Make the victim out as the guilty party?"

"Is that how you see yourself? As a victim?"

Dena opened her mouth—to deny it? to agree? Whatever she'd started to say came out as an irritated huff.

"You can believe whatever you like," Gabe said, "but I was looking forward to spending the day with you. It didn't work out, and for that I'm sorry, but I would've thought as a business owner you'd understand that these things happen." Wearily he scrubbed the back of his neck. "We'd better get inside. You're right. This isn't the place for this."

He moved past Dena, but stopped halfway up the steps when she said his name. Looking back, he saw that she hadn't budged.

"It wasn't that," she said quietly. "That you had to go in to the office. That, I understood."

She looked so vulnerable standing there, so like the unassertive girl he used to know.

"It was that you didn't tell me in person," she said, her voice wobbling a little. "All you had to do was come up to my room and knock on my door."

"It bothered you that much? That I left a note?"

"I felt like a...like an afterthought. Like I didn't matter."

"Dena." Gabe retraced his steps, until he was standing right in front of her. "I got that call at 4:00 a.m. An important case was threatening to blow up in our face—witnesses balking, new evidence turning up.... We had to bolt out of the house right then. Should I have started pounding on your bedroom door at four in the morning?"

She had the grace to look sheepish. "Only if you wanted to see how mad I could really get."

"I figured when you didn't see me at breakfast you'd find my note and still have time to discover a miracle allergy cure and go on that garden thing."

"I didn't come downstairs till after everyone had left," she said.

"Except Scott." *Leave it alone,* he told himself. The last image he wanted to project was that of jealous swain. Lord knew she had a right to watch those damn whales with whomever she chose.

He offered his arm. She hesitated only slightly

before sliding her hand through his elbow, her fingers cool and silky on his skin.

"So," he said, as he ushered her up the steps. "Tell me more about these minkes."

9

DENA FOLLOWED THE SOUNDS of activity to the kitchen. The others were all there, busily preparing the picnic dinner they'd enjoy while listening to the Long Island Philharmonic play classical music under the stars at one of the state parks.

Rhonda was the first to spot the elastic bandage binding Dena's knee. Her hands stilled on the turkey breast she was slicing. "What happened to you?"

"Took a spill off my bike." All eyes on her, Dena limped into the room and slowly eased herself onto a maple chair between Reba and Ham, who were slicing loaves of homemade pumpernickel and whole-grain bread. Frank occupied another chair and was in the process of cutting a wedge of cheddar cheese into chunks. Most of it ended up in his mouth.

That morning a dozen of the hardiest reunion-goers had rented bikes and taken the ferry to Shelter Island, located between the north and south forks of Long Island. There they'd biked the twenty-five-mile butterfly-shaped trail.

Dena and Gabe had paired up and ridden together, which had seemed natural after the night before. Their little tête-à-tête in front of the Harvard Club had been a turning point of sorts. The dinner that followed had been relaxed and fun, with none of the awkwardness that had plagued them since last Saturday.

Almost like old times.

Dena had yet to decide how she felt about that. For that matter, she had yet to decide how she felt about her little subterfuge tonight, but with only one day left before she and Gabe went their separate ways...

"When did you fall?" Scott asked. "I didn't notice."

"I was behind you. It happened when I took that last turn."

"When?" Gabe paused in the act of squeezing lemons into a gallon jug of iced tea. "I was with you the whole time. I never saw you fall."

"Sure you did," Dena said. "I'm not surprised you forgot. It didn't seem like anything at the time, but later my knee started acting up."

"That can happen," Reba said, "delayed reactions like that. You ought to have it looked at. You might have torn something."

"That's what I was thinking," Dena said, rubbing her bandaged knee.

Frowning, Gabe screwed the top onto the tea jar. "I know I never saw you fall."

"It was quick. Remember? Neither one of us thought anything of it at the time." Dena drilled him with a pointed look. "Remember?"

He blinked. "Oh, *that*. Yes, I remember now. You fell. When you took that last turn."

Took you long enough to "remember," Dena thought.

"That's why I didn't go," Andrea said, from the

center island where her delicate little hands were busy wrapping sandwiches in wax paper. "I have too many responsibilities to risk an injury like that."

Oh, is that why you didn't go? Dena was tempted to ask. *I thought it was because you have no stamina or muscle tone.* The natural result of dieting down to a size two and engaging in no physical activity aside from carrying on with other people's boyfriends.

"I hate to cop out on you guys again," Dena said, still rubbing the knee, "but I'm afraid to try to drive like this—not to mention all the walking once we get to the park. And anyway, I really think I'd better get it checked right away," she added, looking meaningfully at Gabe.

Ham, sitting next to her, glanced at her knee, then at her face. Just long enough for her to intercept what could only be called a directorial look. She was familiar with that look but hadn't seen it since high school when Ham had been her drama coach, directing the school production of *Sabrina*. Dena had had the title role, and Gabe had played her love interest—and that was the look Ham used to give them when he wanted more pathos, more fervor, more *feeling*.

Ham was a devotee of Method acting, a technique that requires the actor to internalize the character's personality, to think and feel like the character. At one point when they were rehearsing *Sabrina*, Ham had been unsatisfied with the level of passion Gabe exhibited when he and Sabrina had their Big Kiss. Ham had pulled Gabe off to the side and, for his ears only, had described in graphic detail precisely what he should be thinking about while kissing Sabrina. As he'd listened, Gabe's ears had turned redder and redder. Afterward he'd adamantly refused to tell anyone what Ham had said.

All Dena knew was that from then on, she'd always been eager to rehearse that particular scene.

She didn't know what had prompted Ham to give her that look now, but it had the same effect that it had had back then. Drawing on her recollections of physical pain, she tensed her facial muscles and subtly shifted in her chair as if to find a more comfortable position.

It had to be her imagination, but she could swear Ham bestowed his unspoken approval. Which was impossible. He couldn't know it was a performance.

Could he?

"You don't have to go to the emergency room," Reba said. "There's one of those walk-in places five minutes away. They can X-ray it there and everything."

"But how will she get there," Ham asked, "since Gabe and I have to drive everyone else to the park?" His gaze flicked to Gabe, now absorbed in packing the wicker picnic hamper with food.

Dena waited a few seconds, then said, "Oh, don't be silly. I'll take a cab."

"Gosh, I wish you didn't have to do that," Ham said. And more loudly, "There must be some other way."

Gabe's hands stilled and his head snapped up. Finally catching on. His cluelessness was as sweet as it was exasperating. "I'll take her," he said.

Andrea looked up from her meticulous sandwich wrapping. Her expression was unreadable, but

Dena had the distinct impression Gabe wasn't the only one finally catching on.

"You can't!" Rhonda protested. "How will the rest of us get to the park?"

"We can call Gil again," Ham suggested. "He won't mind."

"Why don't you just borrow my Navigator?" Dena said, producing the keys from the pocket of her boxer-style black-and-white-checked shorts.

Frank made a grab for the keys, but Scott was too fast for him. "I'll put some gas in it," Scott said as he pocketed the keys. "You're running low."

"Well." Rhonda appeared vastly relieved. "That's settled, then."

"WE'RE GOING TO HELL. You know that, don't you?" Dena said as she helped herself to a second slice of pizza. "Yesterday's fibs, and now this."

"A couple of innocent white lies," Gabe said, mouth full. "For a good cause—making up for our missed beach date."

"You're a lawyer. I'm not used to lying."

He affected a wounded look, and warned, "I can still catch the end of the concert, if I hurry."

They were in the family room, a sprawling yet homey space with a whitewashed brick fireplace and an eclectic assortment of furniture arranged in cozy groupings. Gabe and Dena sat cross-legged on tasseled floor pillows on opposite sides of a glass-topped antique steamer trunk that served as a coffee table. The open pizza box was on the floor nearby.

The stereo played Steely Dan's mellow jazz/rock. In a nearby corner were clustered a half dozen fat, vanilla-scented candles in iron floor stands of varying heights. The warm glow they cast was augmented only by one small table lamp.

As soon as the others had left, Dena and Gabe had run out to the video store and discovered that the movie that had once been their mutual favorite still was. They'd munched microwave popcorn while watching *Some Like It Hot*, but that had only sharpened their appetite. After the movie they'd ordered a pizza with their trademark anchovies and fried eggplant.

"I haven't done this much lying since we used to tell my folks we were going to the library to study," Dena said. A blob of melted cheese dropped off her pizza, narrowly missing her pimento-colored silk T-shirt.

"Do you think they ever suspected we were really making out at the duck pond?" Gabe took a pull from his bottle of beer.

"I didn't think so at the time, but a few years later I got up the nerve to ask my mom."

His eyes widened. "What did she say?"

Dena grinned. "She said that back then she figured whatever I was doing that left me with my hair tangled and my cheeks pink, at least I was doing it with you and not some irresponsible boy who didn't respect me. Oh, and she said once I came back from the library with my shirt inside out."

"Oh God," he groaned, and they both laughed.

"I wonder if I'd be capable of that kind of restraint as a parent," Dena said, as she picked at the label of her beer bottle. "Knowing some sort of hanky-panky was going on, but trusting in my daughter's judgment and maturity."

"Your mother's trust was well founded. I still don't know how you kept my adolescent urges reined in for so long."

Gabe looked instantly uncomfortable, as if he'd spoken without thinking. Perhaps he was afraid of jeopardizing their fragile détente by reminding Dena that when he'd finally given in to those adolescent urges, she'd been nowhere in sight.

He needn't have worried. Somehow, for Dena, thinking about what had broken them up no longer hurt as much as it once had. For the past fifteen years, whenever she'd thought about the incident, she'd imagined Gabe as he'd been then, or as her selective memory portrayed him. The Gabe who sat in front of her now was a complex man who had little in common with the boy she'd once known.

Dena gave him a lopsided smile. "You seem to assume you were the only one struggling with those adolescent urges. I had to rein in the both of us."

"Those were incredible, our dates in the back seat of that Camaro. Heaven and hell at once. I used to go home in such pain."

"Everything's so new when you're that age," she said. "So exciting."

Gabe looked pained. "I wish—"

Dena shushed him with a finger to his lips. "Those are the good memories," she said gently. "They're still good memories. They always have been."

He captured her hand and pressed a kiss to her palm, never taking his eyes from hers, his gaze so raw, so heartbreakingly open, it robbed her of speech. He lowered their linked hands to the table.

"I think about what might have been," he said, his voice choked with emotion. "The plans we had…"

She squeezed his hand. "I wonder, sometimes, if we really could've made it work. We were so young."

"But so much in love." His thumb rubbed her knuckles.

"Sometimes love alone isn't enough."

"We sure thought it was, back then." He studied her face. "Why did you do this, Dena? Fake the injury and connive to spend the evening with me?"

What could she say? She didn't know herself. She only knew that they had one day left, that she couldn't go back home with this maelstrom of conflicting emotions swirling inside.

You don't get anywhere without taking risks. Devlin's Second Rule of Business.

Dena rose. Gabe's eyes tracked her progress around the coffee table. She sat next to him, and he scooted over to make room for her on the large floor pillow.

Her heart sprinted. Her breath came fast and shallow. She stared into his whiskey-colored eyes, searching for…what? Some assurance that she was doing the right thing? That she wouldn't curse herself, and him, tomorrow? That she wouldn't regret the reckless impulse that even now made her lean toward him and touch her lips to his?

The connection was nearly electric; an energy seemed to flow between them. This kiss was different from the one they'd shared three days ago in the workshop; different, too, from those they'd stolen in the back seat of Gabe's Camaro so long ago. They both knew where this kiss would take them.

That knowledge both thrilled and terrified Dena. This man had broken her heart once. If she let it happen again, she had no one to blame but herself.

"It's all right," he murmured against her mouth, as if reading her mind. "It's all right, love...."

Dena lifted her hand and caressed Gabe's face, his evening beard shadow like sandpaper under her fingers. He angled his head and deepened the kiss, and eagerly she followed his lead, tasting and touching, filling her senses with him.

She felt her shirt being pulled out of the waistband of her shorts, felt Gabe's big, hot hand stroke up her back. A sigh escaped her. His touch became bolder, sliding around to her breasts, lingering on the sensitive tips straining against her bra. She groaned into his mouth.

"Dena, how I've missed you," Gabe murmured, pressing hard, hungry kisses to her face and throat. He yanked her shirt up and over her head, tossing it aside.

Then he just stared. Dena's bra was flesh-toned lace, accented with contrasting strips of black along the underwire and across the cup seams. The shoulder straps were thin double cords of black satin. The dramatic touches of black emphasized the bra's structure and thus the bounty that filled it to capacity.

Gabe shook his head in wonder. "You never owned anything like this in high school." His thumbs circled Dena's nipples, clearly visible beneath the sheer lace, coaxing them to stiff peaks. "You're so beautiful," he breathed, almost reverently, as his greedy eyes devoured her form before returning to her face. "Even more beautiful than I remembered."

He kissed her again, with searing possessiveness, crushing her to him. Dena felt as if she were floating free of herself, melding with him. He unhooked the bra and drew it away, even as he lowered her to the floor, her back supported by the big pillow. She pulled him down on top of her, delighting in the weight of him, in the way their bodies seemed to fit together like two halves of a matched set.

Gabe kissed a tingling trail down to her breasts. Dena cried out under the bold stroke of his tongue, the hot suction of his mouth. Her fingers pushed through his light brown hair, slid down his thick, corded neck. Her long fingernails dug into his shoulders, but he didn't seem to notice.

Panting, she groaned his name, clung to him tighter. She found herself moving restlessly against him. Without relinquishing her breasts, he slid one hand downward, over her shorts, to caress her intimately.

Dena gasped, arching into his touch, a hairbreadth from release.

In the next instant they lurched apart as voices came from the front of the house, followed by the sound of a door slamming.

Swearing under his breath, Gabe hurled himself at Dena's T-shirt and tossed it to her.

"My bra!" she said, frantically searching for it.

He glanced around. "Do without it."

"*Me?*"

A grin split his face. "Maybe not."

The voices and footfalls were louder. Rhonda called, "Dena? Gabe?"

"Got it!" She snatched the bra from under the coffee table, presenting her back as she shoved her arms through the straps. "Hook it up. Hurry!"

"...acoustically speaking," she heard Andrea say. "But what can one expect from an open-air performance?"

"If sound quality is all you care about, stick to Carnegie Hall." Scott's voice. "There's a lot more to music in the park than music."

"You don't think they could still be at the doctor?" Rhonda asked.

Dena pulled her shirt over her head just as Frank said, "Nah, his car's here."

The double louvered doors swung open and Andrea, Scott, Rhonda and Frank entered the family room.

"There you are!" Rhonda said. "How's the knee?"

"Well, they X-rayed it," Gabe said, leaning negligently on one palm as he lifted a slice of pizza.

His nonchalant performance amazed Dena, who fought to school her expression as her heart stuttered like a Tommy gun. It had to be all those years as a courtroom lawyer, she realized. This was a man who'd never tip his hand by losing his cool.

"No serious damage," Gabe added, "just a mild muscle pull."

"Well, thank God for that," Rhonda said, though she looked at Dena a little oddly, for some reason.

Frank, however, only had eyes for the half-full pizza box. "You gonna eat that?" Peering at it more closely, he grimaced. "What the hell did they put on it?"

Scott picked up the videotape box. "*Some Like It Hot*. Good choice. Marilyn Monroe—my kinda woman." He looked at Dena appraisingly. "I always figured you and she must've been separated at birth."

Dena laughed. "Which would only make me about seventy-three now."

"You *must* be feeling better," Andrea said. "No more bandage. No swelling or discoloration that I can see. And your sense of humor is intact, so one can assume you're not in pain." Her silver-eyed gaze remained as cool and unruffled as a frozen lake.

Another master of courtroom sangfroid. Dena squirmed under Andrea's blatant scrutiny, wishing they'd all just leave.

As if on cue, Scott said, "Let's let these two polish off their dinner in peace. Did I see one last slice of Reba's peach cobbler in the fridge?"

This last comment motivated Frank to hurriedly withdraw, which Dena suspected was Scott's objective. Rhonda said, "Well, I'm pooped. At home my little one gets me up at five-thirty. You'd think I'd enjoy sleeping late this week, but wouldn't you know, I'm up with the sun every morning. Good night, all."

As Rhonda left, they heard Ham and Reba enter the house. Scott said to Andrea, "You still up for that poker game we promised Ham?"

"In a minute. I've got to check my voice mail, make sure everything's under control at work."

Andrea turned to Gabe. "Unless you've already done that?"

Gabe waved off her concern. "They have the number here. I'm not worried."

Andrea's lips thinned, ever so slightly. "Gabe, I was thinking it might not be a bad idea for us to leave in the morning and put in a full day at the office tomorrow."

Leave in the morning? Dena's spirits went into free fall. Until this moment, she hadn't realized how much she'd been counting on having one last day with Gabe.

"You can leave if you want," Gabe told Andrea, "but you'll have to arrange your own transportation. I'm looking forward to that hike tomorrow, and the dinner cruise. I'm staying."

Dena let out the breath she'd been holding.

"Well." Twin spots of color blossomed on Andrea's cheeks. "I'll make my decision after I check my messages." She strode purposefully from the room.

Before leaving, Scott dropped Dena's car keys into her hand. "That's our Dena, always a trendsetter," he said, flicking the exposed label at the back of her T-shirt. "Next thing you know, *everyone*'ll be wearing their shirts inside out. Sweet dreams, guys."

10

"YOU LOOK LIKE you could use this." Dena handed her water bottle to Andrea and watched her drink thirstily.

Their group of fifteen had been hiking in the forest for about an hour. Andrea had started out at the front of the pack with Dena and Gabe, but had dropped farther and farther back until she now trailed behind even Frank. Dena had actually felt sorry for her, shuffling along with a surly expression on her red, sweat-sheened face.

Andrea's once crisp black sleeveless blouse and oatmeal-colored linen walking shorts were now limp and wrinkled. Her back was bent under the weight of the designer leather backpack she'd insisted on bringing. No doubt she'd packed every imaginable kind of survival gear in preparation for their nature walk—everything except the one thing she really could have used: water. Dena herself had made do with a fanny pack for her wallet, lipstick and a jumbo-size Nestlé's Crunch bar, plus her insulated water bottle on a shoulder strap.

"It's this top I'm wearing," Andrea said as she handed back the bottle. "Black absorbs heat. I should've worn something lighter."

Dena didn't bother to correct her. Andrea's suffering had nothing to do with the color of her cloth-

ing and everything to do with her complete lack of
physical conditioning. The only thing that kept her
so skinny, as far as Dena could tell, was obsessive
dieting bordering on an eating disorder. It certainly
wasn't exercise.

Andrea blotted her face with a tissue. "Aren't we
ever going to rest?"

"I'll walk with you," Dena offered, even though
she'd have preferred being up front with Gabe and
the Washingtons.

Their former classmates Daryl Washington and
his wife, Vanessa, had gone on to veterinary school.
The two now shared both a large-animal veterinary
practice and a profound love of nature, which made
them the logical guides on this hike. They pointed
out the different types of trees and other vegetation,
including mountain laurel, soapbush and arrow-
wood. They identified birds by their calls and had
been quick to spy a fox darting through the under-
growth.

"Here," Dena said, "give me the backpack."

Andrea didn't hesitate. Dena slipped her arms
through the straps and hefted the pack onto her
own shoulders. It weighed at least forty pounds.
Laughing, she said, "The woods are full of rocks.
You don't have to bring them with you."

"Very funny," Andrea griped. "It doesn't hurt to
be prepared for emergencies."

Brilliant sunshine arrowed through the canopy of
leaves, creating a living pattern of light and shadow
on the hilly terrain. A brown rabbit leaped over a
fallen tree studded with feathery white fungi, and
disappeared into a cluster of swamp maples, beyond which Dena glimpsed the twinkle of sunlight

on a small pond. Nearby a woodpecker did its jackhammer imitation. Every inhalation brought the myriad scents of living things sprouting and growing and returning to the earth in an unbroken cycle.

Andrea appeared oblivious to it all, her sullen gaze fixed on the path directly in front of her.

Dena saw Gabe, up ahead with the Washingtons, turn and scan the procession of hikers behind him before homing in on her and Andrea. For a moment she thought he might join them at the rear; instead he sent Dena a wry smile, then turned back around and kept walking.

She and Gabe had retreated to their separate beds shortly after the others had walked in on them last night. Rationally Dena acknowledged that this was for the best. Fate had intervened to keep her from making a big mistake. She'd been lucky. Somehow, though, as she squinted past the throng of hikers ahead of her, trying to keep Gabe in sight, she didn't feel so lucky.

"I decided not to go in to the office today after all," Andrea said.

"I figured that out."

"Without a ride, it would've been a hassle." Andrea sighed. "I shouldn't say this, but sometimes I wish Gabe felt more of a commitment to the firm."

Gabe was *born* committed to that firm! Dena bit her tongue.

"Not that we don't share the same vision," Andrea continued, "as close as we are. It's just that he allows himself to get a little distracted sometimes."

Up ahead, Gabe peered into the woods as Daryl pointed. Vanessa made some comment and they all laughed.

Andrea said, "Gabe and I have a very special relationship. It involves every aspect of our lives—personal, professional, social. We know each other better than any married couple I can think of. We've certainly shared as much over the years as most married people do. Well, except for children." Her tone of voice implied that that, too, was just a matter of time.

Dena swallowed a hard knot of despair. It was insane, she told herself, to still care after all this time. To still *let* herself care. Gabe and Andrea connected in so many ways and on so many levels that Dena could never imagine, not being part of the elite world into which they'd been born.

Was this Andrea's way of warning her away from Gabe? Dena wished she could appreciate the irony of that.

"Looks like you're getting that rest you wanted," Dena said, as the group veered off into a clearing for a snack break. She dropped Andrea's backpack at her feet and walked away.

GABE STOOD AT THE RAIL of the *Crystal II*, staring at the inky expanse of Long Island Sound. In the far distance the Connecticut shore glittered like a string of diamonds on black velvet, reminding him that in the morning he'd be returning to his apartment in Greenwich, an affluent Connecticut bedroom community just north of Manhattan.

This four-hour dinner cruise was the grand finale of the weeklong reunion celebration. The *Crystal II* had been chartered by the reunion committee for the exclusive use of the forty or so former classmates and spouses who'd participated in the activities, plus Ham and Reba, who joked about their roles as "chaperons" for the thirty-something crowd.

In the three hours that had elapsed since they'd boarded the boat at 7:00 p.m., they'd enjoyed a sumptuous buffet dinner, free-flowing liquor, and a live band that was now in high gear. The deck reverberated under the feet of those dancing and hollering along to the band's rendition of "Shout!"

If Gabe and Dena weren't so attuned to each other's thoughts and moods, he'd never have noticed that something was wrong. They'd come close to making love last night. Yet today, although she'd been friendly toward him, even affectionate, he'd sensed an underlying reserve, holding him at a distance.

He'd only noticed it after they'd become separated during the hike. After she'd walked with Andrea.

What had they talked about? More to the point, what malignant notions had Andrea planted in Dena's mind? Gabe grimaced, thinking about his law partner. He knew Andrea Pittman inside and out. He probably knew her better than most husbands know their wives. Her ability to manipulate people, facts and the language made her one hell of a lawyer. Unfortunately, she'd never learned to leave those vaunted skills in the courtroom. Her string of failed personal relationships was a testament to that particular learning disability.

Turning from the boat's rail, Gabe searched the crowd for Dena. She wasn't on the dance floor, which was where he'd last seen her, dancing with Scott Cafferty. Which didn't irk him nearly as much as it would have before last night, when Scott had chased everyone out of the family room so Gabe could be alone with Dena.

For all the good it had done them. By then, the moment was lost. He and Dena couldn't be together—the way they both wanted to—with others in the house.

The song ended and all of the couples abandoned the dance floor for the linen-draped tables where dessert, coffee, and liqueurs had been set out. Vanessa Washington approached the band leader, to request a song, Gabe assumed. She looked lovely tonight in an off-the-shoulder emerald-green cocktail dress that enhanced her athletic figure and café noir complexion. When the band leader handed her the microphone, Gabe smiled in anticipation. Vanessa had been the lead singer for Briarfield High's jazz ensemble way back when.

His smile broadened when she started singing a slow, mellifluous love song from the seventies, "The First Time Ever I Saw Your Face." In Gabe's opinion, Vanessa's throaty alto gave Roberta Flack a run for her money. Emotion welled within him as he listened to the simple, heartfelt lyrics. He'd never been able to hear this song without thinking about Dena.

He spied her then, standing alone at the rail some distance away. She wore a body-hugging silver halter dress; her upper arm was encircled by a coiled, topaz-studded silver bracelet. She offered a welcoming smile as he approached her. Without a word, he lifted her hand and led her onto the deserted dance floor. Something akin to panic flashed in her eyes.

"Gabe, no one else is dancing."

"More room for us." He pulled her into his arms and slow-danced her to the center of the clearing. He couldn't help thinking that this was the way they would have danced at the senior prom, if they'd gone. And afterward it would have been just the two of them, sharing their own private dance, binding themselves to each other in the act of love.

Vanessa sent a warm smile their way, still crooning what had to be one of the most romantic songs of all time. Dena glanced around nervously as their former classmates gathered on the sidelines to gawk. Gil Reyes called out, "Objection—counsel is leading the witness!"

"I don't think this is such a good idea," Dena murmured, even as her body moved in time with Gabe's, as if by instinct.

"Since when are you afraid to be the center of attention?"

"There's a difference between drawing attention and making a spectacle of yourself. Don't you think we've given this crowd enough to talk about?"

"No," Gabe said. "Not yet."

He ambushed her with a kiss—the swift, ruthless, take-no-prisoners variety. She stiffened in surprise, and he tightened his hold on her. From the surrounding crowd came shouts and whistles of encouragement.

After a few moments Dena began to relax against him, no doubt sensing that the kiss had run its course and he was about to release her. Instead he cranked it up a notch, pouring everything he had into the kiss, all the passion and yearning he'd kept bottled up for so long. Their audience responded with hooting, foot-stomping applause.

This was kissing as a spectator sport. This kiss made a statement: loud, clear, unambiguous.

Gabe gradually became aware of Dena's arms clinging to him. Of her fingers twined in his hair, her body bowing into his. She returned his kiss with a fervency to match his own, and he felt a tidal wave of triumph surge within him.

Finally he raised his head and stared down into her pink face, into those slumberous green eyes guaranteed to inspire carnal thoughts. Her moist, swollen lips quirked into a lopsided smile.

He said, "Don't believe a word of it."

"Don't believe a word of what?"

Into her ear he said, "Whatever nonsense my esteemed colleague spoon-fed you this morning." In the corner of his vision he glimpsed Andrea sipping a cup of coffee, staring at them poker-faced.

Vanessa was still singing, and other couples began to drift onto the dance floor. Gabe led Dena through the crowd and down the side of the boat next to the enclosed cabin, away from prying eyes and ears. From below came the humming vibration of the diesel engine as the boat headed back to the Island.

Gabe backed Dena against the rail and braced his arms on either side of her, effectively corralling her. Moonlight spilled over her in a river of silver, pooling in the waves of her hair and the folds of her dress. Gabe wanted her so badly it was a physical ache. At that moment he'd have done anything, sacrificed anything, to undo the mistakes of his past.

He took up where he'd left off. "And don't tell

me she didn't feed you some cock-and-bull nonsense, because I know you both better than you think."

Dena reached up and laid cool fingers on his face, her expression sad and tender at once. "She didn't tell me anything I didn't already know."

"Dena. I told you I'm not involved with her. Do you think I lied to you?"

"And I told *you*, it's your private business. It doesn't concern me one way or the other."

He gave her a knowing look. "Even after last night?"

"Gabe—"

"And don't give me any BS about how it never should have happened. A hell of a lot *more* should have happened! And would have, if we hadn't been interrupted. Don't deny it."

She didn't try to.

He pushed off the rail. "So tell me what she said, so I can know how angry to get."

Dena sighed. "None of it was news to me. She told me how close you two are. How your lives are intimately connected, in and out of the firm." She looked away. "How you're almost like a married couple, you know each other so well."

Gabe's bark of laughter snapped her gaze back to him. "That part's true," he chuckled. The dismay on Dena's face prompted him to add, "No, on second thought, the married-couple thing doesn't really fit. Or even a divorced couple. Either of those implies the existence of strong feelings. Which is not the case with me and Andrea."

"Now I know you're lying. How can you not

have strong feelings for the first woman you made love with?"

"I wouldn't call it making love."

Dena rolled her eyes at that. As sincere as the statement was, he knew she construed it as a weaselly attempt to split hairs.

"She told you we're seeing each other?" he asked.

"Well, not in so many words."

"Let me tell you something. Andrea Pittman is a master of linguistic flimflam. She can plant any idea she wants with a well-placed word or a subtle change in inflection." He arched an eyebrow. "Need I add, she's a valuable asset to the firm."

Dena crossed her arms. "What an ego boost that must be for you. Her going to all that trouble to get me out of the picture."

"What, you think she's jealous?"

"What else?"

"I can state with complete confidence that Andrea has no designs on me. Ours is strictly a professional relationship."

"Then why…?"

"*You* were the one she wanted."

"*What?*"

Gabe grinned. "As a client of the firm, that is. She was determined to raid Xanadu away from Gilliam, Shapiro. You infuriated her when you burned her off. Andrea's accustomed to getting what she wants—professionally, that is. I don't think the man's been born who can live with that woman. Lord knows she's gone through enough of them."

"So by laying all that on me about your 'special relationship,' she was just trying to…?"

"Get back at you," Gabe said. "For thwarting her. A tad more restrained than how she chose to punish me fifteen years ago."

Dena frowned. "Punish *you?*"

"By spreading it all around school. About what happened that night."

Dena straightened. "*She* spread it around? I don't believe you!"

"What, you think *I* told everyone what happened? Why would I do a thing like that?" Gabe shook his head, incredulous. "I wanted to forget it ever happened. The last thing I wanted was for you to find out."

Dena looked skeptical. "But why would she let everyone know about it? Her reputation…"

"Well, you might not have been privy to certain, uh, news flashes, never having hung out in the boys' locker room, but let me assure you, by senior year, Andrea's reputation was more or less sealed."

"I kind of knew that. So what was she punishing you for?" Dena asked with a mischievous smile. "Don't tell me you failed to measure up?" At his startled expression she added, "I'm kidding!"

"I know, I just…I'm surprised to hear you joke about it. Surprised and kind of gratified, I guess."

After a few moments she said, "I don't feel the same way about any of this that I used to. Seeing you after all this time, getting to know you as you are now…it's like the sharp edges of my memories have been blunted, rounded off. They don't jab at me the way they once did. Does that make sense?"

"It does to me." He stood close enough to take her in his arms. Instead he kissed her on the forehead, touching her only with his lips. He nodded toward the bow of the boat, where the lights of Long Island crept ever closer. "Looks like we have time for one last dance." He offered his hand and she took it, her smile more crooked than ever.

"So we're actually going to dance this time?" she said, as the band struck up a lively swing number. "You do realize they'll all be watching us like hawks, waiting for us to give them something else to talk about."

"I've got it!" Gabe snapped his fingers. "You could go out there with your dress inside out. Oh wait, you've done that."

"Not funny." Dena gave him a little shove. "Let's stick to public necking."

11

WEARING ONLY SWIM TRUNKS, with a towel slung over his shoulder, Gabe made his way across the moonlit back lawn. The grass felt cool and prickly under his bare feet; the earthy scents of the nearby woods filled his nostrils. He followed the spectral blue-green glow of the free-form swimming pool and the hot tub that protruded from one side of it, barely visible through the surrounding vegetation.

As Gabe stepped onto the flagstone apron his gaze went directly to the hot tub, where Dena, immersed to her bare shoulders in seething water, sat sipping from a glass of white wine. At first glance she appeared to be naked, but closer inspection revealed a strapless metallic aqua swimsuit, shimmering in the cool light from below. The Mermaid Queen in repose.

"You're the picture of decadence," he said, as he tossed his towel on the arm of a chaise. "Is this a bout of solitary hedonism or would you like some company?"

Her wet hair was slicked back off her face, telling him she'd already gone for a swim. She set her wineglass on the flagstone next to a second, full, one. "I was wondering how long it would take you to find me."

It was 1:30 a.m. They'd returned from the dinner

cruise more than two hours earlier. As soon as he'd ascertained that the rest of the household was safely asleep, Gabe had crept up to Dena's room and found it deserted.

He stepped into the hot tub and settled on the bench across from her. A groan of pleasure rumbled up his throat as he was enveloped by steaming water, churned to a froth by jets in the wall of the tub. Dena smiled and handed him the other glass. Their bare legs touched underwater. The wine etched a frosty path down his throat, in startling contrast to the delicious heat pummeling his body. Outside their little oasis, darkness stretched in all directions.

Dena said, "You never answered my question, you know." At his quizzical expression she added, "Why did Andrea make sure everyone, including me, knew about you and her and the golf course? What was she punishing you for?"

Gabe took another sip of his wine and set down the glass. "I feel it only fair to warn you, you're coming perilously close to hearing the dreaded *explanation*. The whole enchilada. One detail leads to another."

She draped her arms over the edge of the tub, staring at him expectantly. "Maybe I'm ready for the whole enchilada."

The enormity of it slammed into Gabe, stealing his voice. She wanted to hear it. All of it. Now that the long-awaited moment had come, he found himself battling a rising panic. He was about to strip himself bare, dredge up the most shameful episode of his life and spread it in all its ignominy before the only woman he'd ever loved.

What had made him think this was a good idea?

Her expectant expression faltered. "You don't want to."

"I want to." Gabe snatched up his wineglass and drained it. "I just don't know where to start."

Her gentle smile radiated so much empathy and affection, Gabe could only marvel at his own baseless fears.

This was his Dena. Everything would be all right.

He decided to plunge into it headlong. "It was April of our senior year. Dad's firm was having this wingding at the Briarfield Country Club, to honor a senior associate who was retiring. It was the first time I'd been invited to one of their formal functions. Andrea, too. I mean everyone knew we both planned to go to law school and join the firm eventually, but this was sort of our...coming out, you might say."

"And you wanted to make a good impression."

She was so sweetly understanding, Gabe felt instantly humbled.

"Yeah," he said. "I really did. This was my first opportunity to hobnob with these people who would be important to my career later on. The partners. The associates. Even the summer interns." He took a deep breath. "My parents had been hectoring me for weeks to escort Andrea to this thing. I mean she was going anyway, but they thought we should go as a couple."

Dena frowned. "Even though they knew you and I were seeing each other exclusively? Even though I'd been a guest in their *home?*"

Her incredulity triggered a rush of shame for his parents' crass behavior. He knew that Dena's folks,

Mimi and Carl Devlin, would never have lowered themselves in such a way.

"They badgered me," he said, "but I can't lay the blame on them. I made my own decision. It was supposed to be a onetime occurrence, this 'date,' strictly platonic. The way I had it figured, it wouldn't have affected you and me at all."

"Because I wasn't supposed to find out." She sounded resigned rather than angry.

Gabe made himself say, "That's right. You weren't supposed to find out." He allowed himself a mirthless chuckle. "It's amazing what you can rationalize when you're young and stupid."

"And arrogant," she said with a half smile.

"Well, that goes without saying. I talked myself into it really, trying to salve my conscience. It was for *your* benefit, you see."

"Of course," she said dryly.

"I told myself I was sparing your feelings by not taking you to that snobby affair, where you'd have had to socialize with a whole passel of people as stuffy and intimidating as my parents. You were pretty scared of them, as I recall."

"I was scared of a lot. I got over it. Andrea told me that when you asked her to be your date you said something to the effect that I was out of the picture—'out of the equation,' that's how she put it. And that she assumed we broke up."

"I don't remember saying anything like that, but I might've—I was feeling so guilty and conflicted about the whole thing. I know I didn't tell her you and I had broken up. I didn't want her getting the wrong idea. She'd had kind of a crush on me for a long time. Well, more than a crush really. She'd bought in to this whole marriage idea our parents were forever shoving down our throats. To her, I was part of the package she was entitled to, along with the Harvard sheepskin and the corner office at Moreau Pittman."

"So you ask this girl who thinks she's going to *marry* you out on a date, and you expect her not to get 'the wrong idea'?" Dena splashed water in Gabe's face. "You men can be so *dense!*"

"Thank you."

"We both know you didn't leave me back home in Dogpatch to spare my feelings. You were embarrassed by me."

Something tightened hard in his gut, stealing his breath. "Dena, I was never embarrassed by you. I…" *Don't start prevaricating now*, an inner voice warned. *You've come too far.* "The thing is, I had to concentrate on my performance that night. I was going to be 'on,' laying the foundation for my future. At least that's how I saw it. I had to be focused, and I knew I couldn't do that if I was…distracted."

"Worried about what I would say or do, you mean."

Gabe picked up his wineglass, discovered it was empty, and set it down again.

Dena said, "For all you knew, I might even have answered honestly if one of your parents' snooty friends asked me what line of work my father was in. 'Oh, he's a janitor at the high school. He has his name on his uniform and everything!'"

Gabe sank lower in the water. She'd read his mind.

"You must've been worried about what I'd wear, too." A gust of laughter burst from Dena. "With good reason. My sense of fashion is one thing that hasn't changed much over the years."

"You're incredible," he said. "Why aren't you biting my head off?"

"I'm saving my appetite." She trailed her fingers through the warm bubbles. "Poaching you first. There was something else Andrea said...."

"Oh God."

Dena smiled. "You were very 'persuasive' out on that golf course. A regular Don Juan."

Gabe straightened. "That is such a load of—"

"I didn't believe it, of course."

"You didn't?"

"I mean, I did at first, but later, when I had a chance to think about it, it just didn't add up. The girls used to talk, too, you know. Everyone knew Andrea was experienced. And you weren't. Oh, don't look at me like that! I'm not saying you weren't sexy. You were sexy, Gabe, you were horny, you were as inventive in the back seat of that Camaro as my pants-on rule allowed, but let's face it. You were no Don Juan."

He slumped back. "When are we getting to the good part?"

"I figure there's a better-than-even chance the golf course wasn't your idea."

"Darn right it wasn't. About two-thirds of the way through that shindig Andrea produces this bottle of Dom Perignon she sweet-talked the bartender out of and says let's you and me find a quiet spot and decompress for a few minutes. The stress was getting to us both."

"So like a lamb to the slaughter, you meekly follow the self-appointed future Mrs. Moreau out to the dark and deserted golf course."

Now it was Gabe's turn to splash water at Dena. "Do you want to hear the rest of this or what?"

"You can skip over the juicy parts."

"I don't remember any juicy parts, although I suppose there must have been some. By the time we got down to it, I was so sozzled it was a wonder I could do anything at all."

"So she plied you with alcohol and took advantage of you, is that it?"

"Stop smirking. I take full responsibility for my actions. She was very aggressive, as I recall, and determined as hell, but at some point I must've made a decision to go along with it. It was a bottle of bubbly she was wielding, not a gun."

"And after?" Dena asked quietly.

Gabe sighed. "After...I despised myself. You wonder why I meekly followed Andrea, why I didn't realize what she was up to. It all comes back to this youthful arrogance, this absolute confidence in my ability to handle the situation—to handle *her*." He threw up his hands in mock dismissal of the danger. "She was a *girl*. I could handle a girl!"

"Oh brother," Dena chuckled. "'Come out to my golf course,' said the spider to the fly."

Gabe leaned across the hot tub, filched Dena's glass off the flagstone and drained it. "Hey!" she laughed.

The heat and wine conspired to turn Gabe to jelly. He couldn't recall ever having felt so extravagantly relaxed. "At this point we come back to the question that started it all," he intoned, steepling his fingers. "Why did Andrea want to punish me?"

Dena waved her hand vigorously. "Oh, I know! I know! Call on me!"

Gabe pointed. "The moist young lady in the mermaid outfit."

"Because hell hath no fury like a woman scorned?"

"Trite but true. Once I'd made it clear there'd be no repeat performance, and zero chance of us tying the knot, Andrea became vindictive as hell. The first person she told was Rhonda Peterson."

Dena's eyes widened. "She doesn't fool around!"

"By third period I was fielding golf jokes from every guy I knew and half the teachers." He sobered. "I can imagine what you went through."

"I thought it was you who spread it around. You know, bragging about your conquest."

"I didn't tell a soul. I was just praying you wouldn't find out. Not very noble, but I didn't want to lose you. And God knows I never wanted to hurt you."

Gabe leaned forward and looked her in the eye. He reached for her hands underwater and held on to them. "I'm so sorry, Dena. I never got a chance to tell you that. I'm so damn sorry for all of it."

Her eyes welled with tears. She looked down. "I should've let you explain. Back then, when you wanted to."

"You weren't ready. And like I said, if the roles were reversed, I wouldn't have been so keen to hear your side, either."

"It was such a crushing blow at the time. Now, hearing about it, about everything that led up to it…I don't know, it's like it's been demystified. Defanged. It's easier now to see what you did as a youthful indiscretion—something that could've happened to anyone."

"Maybe that's due to the passage of time, the emotional distance you've gained. After all, I've been nothing to you for fifteen years."

In a small voice she said, "That's not true. I've never stopped missing you, Gabe. I've never felt the same way about any other man."

He squeezed her hands. Speaking around a lump in his throat, he said, "Not even the fiancé? The one who cheated on you?"

"Not even him. I think I convinced myself I loved him. It's just as well it didn't work out."

He said, "Losing you was like…like having someone close to me die. And it was all my fault. I was stunned, shell-shocked. For the first time in my life, I had to face the fact that I'd screwed up big time, and nothing I could do was going to make it better."

"I was only thinking of my own pain at the time. I had no idea you were suffering, too."

"Ultimately that suffering was a positive thing," he said. "Not pleasant, or welcome, but necessary. I could no longer close my eyes to what I was turning into."

"Which was…?"

"A clone of my father. I found myself exhibiting the same calculating, self-serving mind-set. The same callous elitism. I was disgusted by the way I'd treated you, intentionally shutting my future bride out of a part of my life that was bound to be important to both of us someday—my career. I made a conscious decision at that point—a vow to myself—not to live my life that way."

Dena was studying him intently. "And did you keep your vow?"

Gabe nodded. "After I lost you I knew I could no longer walk in my father's footsteps. Not that he's some kind of monster, he's just not the man I want to be."

"It's interesting. The process of self-examination you describe sounds a lot like what Scott says he went through. Losing Annie became a springboard to discovering his religious calling."

"I guess sometimes it takes a tragedy to teach you something about yourself. In my case I ended up with a whole different outlook on relationships, goals, everything. That's the good news. The bad news is it came at a terrible price." Gabe searched Dena's glistening eyes. "Not a day has passed that I haven't thought of you, that I haven't wished to God I could turn back the clock."

She smiled and a tear rolled down her cheek. "Maybe we were meant to split up back then. I'm not the same person I was, and neither are you. Maybe we were meant to find each other when the time was right."

Gabe brushed away her tear with his thumb. "I love you, Dena. I've never stopped loving you." He cupped her face. "I always have and I always will."

She touched her fingers to his lips. "Don't say that, Gabe. It's too soon. Don't even think about always."

He wanted to think about it. He wanted to talk about it, plan it, live it, shout it from the rooftops. His *always* with Dena. Instead he slid off the bench and knelt in the warm, churning water. She didn't object when he parted her legs and moved between them. He pressed weightless kisses to her cheeks, and a lingering one on her mouth. She tasted like wine and tears and hope.

His lips found her ear. "It's prom night."

12

DENA'S FINGERS TANGLED in Gabe's hair. She kissed him with a blind intensity that frightened her.

Prom night.

Words heavy with private meaning, ripe with promise. For fifteen years Dena had wondered how it would have been if she and Gabe had made love on prom night, as they'd planned. If they'd been each other's first. And last.

Their arms locked around each other and she found herself slipping off the bench, kneeling belly to belly with Gabe on the smooth floor of the hot tub as steaming water surged and pulsed around them.

Would the anticipation have been this wondrous fifteen years ago? This perfect?

Probably not. What she'd said was true. They were different people now.

The kiss took on a life of its own as Gabe's tongue thrust and retreated, fueling Dena's arousal. The solid ridge of his erection pressed against her belly, and she seized his buttocks, pulling him closer still.

Gabe broke off, breathing hard. Dena gulped air, filling her lungs with the perfume of the flowering shrubs that surrounded the pool and guarded their privacy. He stood, pulling her to her feet. The water came to midthigh.

"Stay here," Gabe said. He stepped out of the tub, plucked a pale flower from a nearby bush and returned to her. He held it under her nose, and she inhaled its lush scent. Not being a plant person, she had no idea what variety it was.

"Every girl needs a corsage for her prom," he said, and tucked the blossom behind her ear.

She touched the petals, softer than the finest velvet. He pulled her into his arms as he had earlier that evening aboard the *Crystal II*. They started dancing, moving in a small circle in the hot tub.

Dena rested her head on Gabe's shoulder. Crickets trilled. Somewhere far away a dog barked. She sighed. "They're playing our song."

"I tipped the band." His hand glided down her back and rested lightly on her bottom.

After a long moment she murmured, "Gabe? Are we going to regret this?"

"No." He made her look him in the eye. "I've never felt anything so right. You feel it. I know you do."

She couldn't deny it.

Gabe grasped the top of her strapless swimsuit and pulled it down to her waist. Pale moonlight from above and the unearthly glow from the tub combined to cast the angles of his face in sharp relief. His hair was disheveled and his eyes glowed even in shadow as he stared at her, giving him a predatory appearance that sent of shiver of excitement through her.

He bent and placed a soft kiss on the tingling, pebbled tip of one breast. Dena clutched his shoulders, dizzy with desire. His scalding mouth closed over the nipple and she bit back a cry. The leisurely, rhythmic tugging of his mouth, the teasing stroke of his tongue, drove her to the edge of madness.

She uttered pleas, and oaths, and desperate, keening sounds with an eloquence all their own. He kissed his way to the other side, in no hurry, as if savoring every second. He suckled her with mounting urgency, and bit gently, wringing sharp little gasps of delight from her.

Dena slid her hand down his torso and under the drawstring waistband of his swim trunks, shocked by her boldness. She and Gabe had never touched below the waist back when they were dating. She closed her fingers around his penis and felt the hot, hard thickness of it buck impatiently. Gabe jerked as if burned. The breath left his lungs in one long, guttural groan.

He stripped off his trunks and tossed them onto the flagstones. Her swimsuit followed, and he hurled it away without taking his eyes from her. It plopped into the pool and sank to the bottom.

Gabe held her at arm's length and looked at her, all of her. "You take my breath away." He growled in frustration. "I wanted to go slow for you, but, love, I've got to tell you, I don't think I can wait much longer."

"Oh, good." She hurled herself at him and kissed him soundly on the mouth. "We can go slow next time." Another kiss. "Or the time after that." She kissed him as he lifted her and wrapped her legs around his hips. "Or the third time or the fourth or—" The rest was lost on a sharp gasp as he lowered her onto his erection, filling her in one long, slow thrust.

Gabe hadn't lied. Nothing had ever felt so right.

The look of wonder on his face no doubt mirrored her own. As one, they smiled, and no words were needed. Their bodies receded and came together in an unhurried rhythm as Gabe stepped out of the hot tub and carried Dena to a flat green chaise, which looked black in the moonlight. With their bodies still intimately joined, he lowered them both to the tufted canvas cushion.

The steel body of the chaise creaked as the cadence of their loving escalated, inching across the flagstones in time to their movements. Dena clung to Gabe's back, digging her fingers into the ridges of muscle along the valley of his spine. He kissed her fiercely, gripping her hard as he lunged fast and deep.

Breathless cries heralded her climax; at that moment she didn't care if she woke the whole house. Gabe watched her intently, as if relishing every nuance of her expression. She fell apart, shattered with the explosive force of her orgasm. He held her tight, stoking it, prolonging it, even as he yielded to his own hammering release.

Yes, Dena thought, as they clung to each other, breathless, spent. Nothing had ever felt so right.

13

"DID YOU LEAVE anything at home?" Gabe lifted a heavy leather suitcase into the back of Dena's sport utility vehicle, fitting it next to the two other suitcases, shoe-filled trunk and swollen cosmetics tote he'd placed there earlier. He wiped his brow. He didn't mind a little exercise, but he preferred the workout he'd gotten last night with Dena.

"I like to have a choice," she said. Today's choice was a short, stretchy skirt in a bright floral pattern, topped with a scoop-necked, sleeveless lime-green tunic in some silky, clingy fabric. Around her throat was a choker comprised of an eclectic assortment of exotic-looking glass beads. More beads hung from the necklace on knotted leather cords of varying lengths that formed a V-shaped curtain, the very tip of which nestled in her cleavage. Gabe's eyes kept straying to that bottom bead.

"Can you drive in those things?" He gestured toward her towering lime-green patent-leather mules.

"I drive barefoot."

"Is that legal?"

"Beats me," she said as she leaned into the vehicle, arranging her luggage. The beaded cords of her necklace swung free, tinkling like wind chimes.

Ham called to Dena as he descended the steps of

the full-length front porch, carrying her bulging garment bag. "Think you brought enough clothes for a week?"

"She likes to have a choice," Gabe said.

"Ham, what are you doing?" Dena rushed over to their old friend and tried in vain to grab the bag away from him. "Are you crazy?" she shrieked. "Think about your heart!"

Reba was right behind him. "What about his heart?"

"Yeah, Ham." Gabe stifled a smile as he watched Ham glance nervously at Reba. "What about your heart? I hope you've been taking those pills."

Reba's eyes narrowed as she watched Ham easily swing the ponderous garment bag into the back of the vehicle and shove it firmly between the other pieces of luggage. She turned to the others. "Okay, what has the old fool been up to now?"

Dena gaped at Ham, hands on hips. "He told us he has a heart condition!"

"I never said that! If you came to that erroneous conclusion, don't blame me."

Reba obviously knew him well. "'Erroneous conclusion,' huh? Have you no shame?"

"Don't yell at me," Ham said. "I'm an old man."

Reba crossed her arms. "With the ticker of a thirty-year-old marathon runner, according to Dr. Bloom."

"You're still a hell of an actor," Gabe said, grinning. "You had both of us fooled."

Reba threw her hands in the air. "I'm not even going to try to guess the reason for this charade."

"He wanted Gabe and me to stay here for the week," Dena said, her expression softening. "Both

of us. Which we weren't inclined to do at the time—
at least I wasn't. So he guilted us into it with this
whole song and dance about declining health, mental confusion…"

"Uh-huh," Reba said, nodding sagely. "Suspiciously similar to the part he played last season in a
local theater production. He was so convincing he
ended up on the mailing lists of three nursing
homes and a cemetery."

Ham spread his hands. "So I reprised a success-
ful role. So sue me. The important thing is it
worked."

He knows, Gabe thought. The old man's eyes were
twinkling, for crying out loud! Last night, after Gabe
had taken a bracing dip in the pool to retrieve
Dena's swimsuit, they'd crept back into the house
and up the stairs to her room. There they'd made
love until dawn—first in the antique canopied four-
poster and later in the luxurious shower whose
multiple nozzles sprayed their bodies from all directions.

Gabe would have sworn no one had gotten wind
of their clandestine activities, yet here was their old
teacher and drama coach, fairly bursting with pride
over the success of his little subterfuge.

Andrea emerged from the house, towing her
wheeled suitcase and carrying her overstuffed
black leather briefcase. She consulted her Patek
Philippe watch. "Gabe, I was hoping to be on the
road an hour ago. At this rate we won't get to the office until noon."

"I'm not going to the office," Gabe said. "I'm going home, after I drop you at your place." Andrea
owned an elegant, ultramodern home in the town

of Larchmont in Westchester County, north of New York City, where both her parents and Gabe's had moved after their children had finished high school.

Her eyes bulged. "But we've lost so much time away from work!"

"It's called a vacation," he said, trying not to lose patience with his workaholic colleague in front of the others. She'd stayed out there all week not for relaxation, but for the opportunity to sniff out former classmates who'd done well for themselves and hit them up as potential clients. With a tone of finality Gabe added, "If you want a ride, I'm leaving after lunch."

She opened her mouth as if to challenge him, then snapped it shut, spun around and wrestled her suitcase back into the house.

Ham muttered, "I always thought that girl was wound a little tight."

"Did you tell them our news?" Reba asked him.

"I wanted us to do it together." He slid his arm around her and announced, "This little schemer has finally persuaded me to marry her."

Dena shrieked in delight.

"Oh, you!" Reba mock-punched him on the arm. "You've been trying to get me to say yes for ages. I only gave in because I could no longer stand to see a grown man beg."

"I'm so happy for you!" Dena cried, giving them both a huge hug.

Gabe slapped Ham on the back and kissed Reba's plump cheek. "That's the best news I've heard in a long time. When's the wedding?"

"As soon as possible," Ham declared. "Next weekend."

"Think again," Reba said. "I want my daughters to be joint matrons of honor, and they need some advance notice. Miriam lives in Chicago, and Rachel is in San Francisco."

"Well, get them out here!" Ham said. "The sooner we get married, the sooner we can have our wedding night." He wagged his brows salaciously, despite the fact that he and Reba had been living together for months. "Just promise you'll be gentle with me, darling."

"Oh, I'll be real gentle with you," Reba said. "As in separate beds. Wouldn't want to aggravate that *heart condition*, would we?"

Ham turned to Gabe and Dena. "You see the trouble you've caused? If you'd just worked it all out fifteen years ago, I wouldn't have to put up with this abuse right now."

"At the risk of giving this old buttinsky here a swelled head," Reba said, "I'm really quite pleased he tricked you into staying all week. Especially you, Gabe—I know it was a last-minute decision for you."

"Last minute?" Dena frowned. "I assumed Ham invited you weeks ago, like he did me."

"He, uh, did," Gabe said. "I accepted only for Saturday night. Didn't want to take a whole week away from work."

"So when did you change your mind?" she asked.

He sighed. "Last Saturday at the kick-off dinner, if you must know, as soon as you told me how much you were looking forward to spending the whole damn week getting caught up with Scott Cafferty."

Dena crossed her arms, smiling. "You were jealous."

"Which couldn't possibly have been your intention." Gabe raised his voice a few octaves and batted his eyelashes. "'He doesn't look like any pastor I've ever met.'"

"Gee," Dena said dryly, "sounds just like me."

Ham winked at Gabe. "That must've been when you slipped over to me and asked if the weeklong invitation was still open."

"So that's the real reason you had to go back to the office for your paperwork," Dena said. "Because you hadn't planned to stay. You must've had to go by your apartment for clothes, too."

"You're looking very pleased with yourself," Gabe grumbled.

"She's allowed," Reba said, and gave Ham a firm shove. "Now, get in the kitchen and help me with the chicken salad, and I'll *think* about having that wedding sometime this year."

"Tyrant!" Ham was grinning as he and Reba disappeared into the house.

"I really am thrilled for Ham," Dena said as she closed up the car. "He's been alone too long."

So have I, Gabe thought, though he knew his fifteen years couldn't compare to Ham's forty.

He pulled her into his arms. "I meant what I said this morning, Dena. We're going to keep seeing each other. A lot. It isn't that far from Greenwich to your place in Jersey."

"We're really limited to weekends, though," she said, "what with the hours you work...."

"I'll cut back if it means I can spend more time with you."

Her smile was melancholy. "That's how you feel now."

"And that's how I'm going to keep feeling."

After a long moment she said, "Let's just concentrate on the present, Gabe. With no expectations. Enjoy what we have for now."

Gabe's frustration warred with his desire to be patient for Dena, to give her the time she needed to overcome her understandable wariness. Last night she'd told him that she'd never felt the same way about any other man, that the time was right for them to be together. But it was clear she didn't fully trust those gut feelings, and for that he took full responsibility. Fifteen years ago she'd given him the precious gift of her love and her trust, and the self-important brat he'd been then had failed to recognize the treasure he held. It was now up to Gabe to prove himself worthy of that which he'd squandered so long ago, and he intended to do just that.

But nothing could change the fact that he and Dena were still light-years apart in ways that he knew she considered crucial. They were from different worlds, and that difference was reflected in everything from their families to their chosen careers to the friends they cultivated and the leisure activities they pursued. However, he was confident that in time, everything would work out.

He ignored the little voice in his head that said, *You thought that fifteen years ago, too.*

Everything *would* work out. It had to.

He couldn't lose her twice.

Gabe took her hand and started around the house to the workshop. "Come with me. You left something in my luxurious lodgings."

"Oh no! I was sure I packed everything. What is it?"

"You'll see." He led her up the steps of the breezeway. Once inside the workshop, he crossed to the windowsill where he'd left the little sack from the antiques store. He handed it to her.

Dena emitted a soft gasp. "Oh. My pug." Her eyes were misty as she drew the figurine out of the bag, with the reverence usually reserved for a holy relic. She set the little black dog on her palm and stared into its tiny, sad-looking face.

God, he loved that lopsided smile of hers. He wanted to see it every day. He wanted to wake up to it. He wanted to bring that smile to her face fifty years from now when she was as wrinkled as one of her beloved pugs.

"I know you said you wouldn't accept it," Gabe said, "but I was hoping you might reconsider."

Dena clutched the figurine to her bosom. "Gabe, I shouldn't have turned it down—"

"No." He raised a palm. "You didn't feel right about it then. I understood that. But that was before…everything." He chuckled. "It's been a hell of a week, love."

"You're telling me?" Dena put her arms around his neck and kissed him on the mouth. "Thank you for Horace."

He grinned. "You named it after your first pug? How do you know it's not a Mildred?"

She turned the figurine over and examined it. "You know, I think you're right."

Gabe took the little statue from her and set it on the worktable. He started to put his arms around Dena, but paused to face the pug away from them.

"Mildred's too young to witness this," he said.

"I thought she was an antique."

"She's led a very sheltered life. Now, I believe you were in the process of thanking me." He nuzzled her neck; the scent of her went to his head like a drug. "Just how appreciative are you?"

She curled her arms around his waist, pressed her voluptuous body against him. "Pretty darn appreciative."

His physical reaction was instantaneous, despite their long hours of loving. Gabe knew he'd never get enough of this woman. "Is that so?" His hand strayed to her breast.

Dena looked at her watch. "When is lunch?"

"Whenever we get there." He abandoned her for the scant seconds it took to draw the shades on the windows and lock the door. Once their privacy was assured, he wasted no time in divesting Dena of her tunic.

Oh, yes. This bra was even more outrageous and enticing than the one she'd worn Thursday. It was lavender, made of some sheer, iridescent material. The front dipped all the way down to a pearl-studded clasp. The tops of the cups were abbreviated, exposing a good portion of her ample breasts.

He flicked the beads of her necklace, which sparkled in the sunlight streaming from the overhead skylight. "Keep this on. It makes you look wild. Primitive. I can pretend you're some kind of pagan princess."

She grinned. "We've been lovers less than twelve hours and already you're getting kinky."

Gabe pulled her to him, sliding his hands to her bottom. She moaned deep in her throat as he caressed her through the tight, stretchy skirt. And again when he took her mouth in a deep, voracious kiss. She moved against him, and he groaned, too, digging his fingers into her fanny, instinctively forcing her hard against his erection as if to penetrate her through their clothing.

He relinquished her mouth and pressed tender kisses down her throat to the hollow under her collarbone, which he'd long ago discovered was one of her many erogenous zones. She shivered and arched into him.

Gabe moved his hands lower, to the short hem of her skirt. He pulled it up a little and stroked the backs of her thighs, bunching the skirt ever higher as his exploration continued. Dena's breathing quickened. She kissed his jaw, nibbled on his ear. There was a surprise in store for him when his hands closed over her bare bottom.

"You're not wearing panties!"

She chuckled. "I'm wearing panties."

Further investigation revealed a silky band of fabric disappearing between her cheeks. Thong panties!

"I have to see this," he said, shoving her skirt all the way up to her waist. "Oh yes." He walked around her for the full effect—funky necklace, high-heeled mules and all—as she laughed and reached back to unzip her skirt. "Yes, I like this," he said. "I like this a lot."

Soft and rounded where most women wanted to be hard and flat, Dena was full-figured but fit, and she looked absolutely sensational in the eensy-teensy thong, which matched her bra. The triangle of tawny hair was clearly visible through the sheer wedge of material in front.

"I wear thongs to avoid a panty line," she explained as she wriggled out of the skirt—a riveting spectacle in itself. "But mostly because they're fun and sexy." She tossed the skirt aside and struck a come-and-get-me pose with upraised arms and a devilish grin.

More than ready to come and get her, Gabe whipped off his T-shirt and kicked off his deck shoes. His fingers went to the fly of his khaki slacks, but Dena stopped him with a throaty "Let me."

She unfastened his pants and let them fall. Her hand closed over him through his white briefs, sliding down the length of him, cupping him lower. She dragged her long, frosted purple fingernails lightly all the way to the tip, making his lungs seize up and his brain melt.

Dena hooked her thumbs into the elastic waistband and worked the briefs over the straining column of his erection. He kicked his clothes away and reached for the front of her bra. It took him a few seconds to figure out the overengineered clasp, and then the bra went flying in the general direction of the rest of their clothes.

The beaded-curtain necklace, earthy in a hip kind of way when she was clothed, looked downright erotic spread out above the creamy abundance of her pink-tipped breasts, which drew his hands like magnets.

"If I'd known back then how incredible making love to you would be," Gabe said, as he stroked the satiny mounds and teased the nipples to points, "I'd never have agreed to wait even one day."

"It was pretty amazing," Dena agreed. She pushed her fingers through his chest hair and teased his flat nipples with her nails.

"It'll keep getting better," he promised.

She didn't respond, and he knew better than to pursue the subject of their future. She wasn't ready.

"Starting now," he added as he hauled her to him and kissed her with a fierce, hot urgency more eloquent than words. He couldn't have kept his hands still if his life had depended on it. This was Dena, his Dena, the woman he'd fantasized about for fifteen years, the woman he'd never stopped loving, and here she was, soft and pliant in his arms, naked but for the bizarre necklace and a microscopic scrap of lavender silk and the kind of shoes that scream, *Take me now!*

His hands glided down her back to the enticing dip of her waist and then on to that luscious bottom. She moved restlessly under his heated touch, making little panting sounds that threatened his sanity.

Her nostrils were flared, her lips slightly parted. He slid his hand down her belly and tickled her sensitive navel. Dena bit her lower lip, clutching him, as if she'd crumple without his support. His fingers slipped under the edge of her panties and lower to graze the soft curls. Her hips rocked in response.

Gabe teased her for another minute or so, slowly stroking the downy mound of her femininity but going no further. She writhed in his embrace, mindlessly seeking relief. Her pupils were dilated, her face and chest flushed pink with her arousal. Her nails gouged his shoulders and he smiled, delighting in her loss of control, in his ability to make her forget everything but the relentless, sharp-edged craving that only he could satisfy.

"Are you ready?" he murmured, prolonging the sensual torment.

"Gabe," she panted, "please..." She grasped his wrist and tried to make him deepen the caress. He chuckled and resisted, and she cheerfully cursed him. Her hand sneaked below his waist, but he caught it before she could secure her target, knowing if he let her touch him there, she'd have the upper hand. So to speak.

"Tell me," he insisted. "Are you ready?"

"*Am I ready?* I've been ready since you pulled down the first window shade! Now, what are you going to do about it?"

Gabe slid one finger lower, pushing through the damp curls to lightly touch her clitoris. She cried out as if in pain. Her hips recoiled, and he tightened his hold on her. Parting the swollen petals, he nudged the delicate opening with a fingertip.

Popular wisdom held that every woman had a special place in her heart for her first lover. Though Gabe was perilously close to the limit of his control, he was determined to make Dena forget whoever it was who'd claimed her innocence—the man who'd taken Gabe's rightful place in her bed and her body and her heart.

Dena pushed against his questing finger. He obliged her, with short, shallow strokes that only served to madden them both. Finally he burrowed his finger deep, deeper, and felt the answering ripple of her intimate muscles. His thumb brushed the tiny center of her sensation, and she sobbed her pleasure, breathless.

"I—I've never been this—" she gasped. "It's never been like this for me."

"Good," he whispered, and softly kissed her mouth, her half-closed eyes.

Gabe withdrew his hand and pulled the panties over her hips to puddle at her feet. She wobbled a little, lust-drunk, and grabbed his shoulders to keep from toppling. He backed her against the plywood worktable and lifted her onto the edge of it. In the brilliant sunlight from above, with the leather-and-bead necklace draped over her chest, she did indeed look like some kind of golden pagan princess. He was certain he'd never seen anything so beautiful.

She wriggled on the unfinished wood. "Is this what they call rough sex?"

"You know the old song—love is a many-splintered thing. Is it really uncomfortable?"

Dena leaned back on her palms. "Something tells me you're about to take my mind off it."

Gabe answered her with a slow, silky smile. He knelt on the plank floor and draped her legs over his shoulders, taking a moment first to remove her shoes. "In the interest of safety," he said. His back and shoulders were already a landscape of claw marks. God only knew what damage stiletto heels could do.

He brushed his fingertips over the slippery folds. Dena's chest rose and fell faster. Gently he spread her. She trembled, watching him. Waiting. At the first touch of his mouth she jerked back with a strangled gasp.

He held her still, indulging himself, varying the pressure of his lips, the stroke of his tongue, now light and fluttery, now firm and probing. Her hoarse cries and her frenzied movements fueled his hunger. The seductive womanly scent of her inflamed him.

When Gabe sensed her climax was nearly upon her he pulled back, deliberately thwarting her, knowing that the longer he held her on that razor edge of sensation, the more intense it would be when she came. Ignoring her whimpers of protest, he kissed her thighs and her belly, lightly blew on her drenched flesh, caressed her everywhere but there.

When she had calmed somewhat he resumed the intimate kiss, only to stop short once more. Laughing, she tried to force his head down. "Trust me," he said. Her response was a frustrated growl. The third time he didn't stop. It took her scant seconds to reach the precipice, and she tumbled over it with a vengeance, bucking up off the table. Those in the house had to hear her rhythmic screams, he thought, but damned if he cared.

Her climax went on and on, and he employed every skill in his repertoire to prolong it. At last she collapsed onto the table, limp and winded, mewling like a kitten. Rising, Gabe struggled with the nearly overpowering impulse to take her right there. But he didn't.

This time was for Dena. He wanted to make it memorable. He wanted to ensure that when she returned to her home in New Jersey, to her solitary bed, her thoughts and dreams would be filled with the phantom imprint of his hands and his mouth, the inexpressible rapture of his body driving into hers. The irrefutable certainty of his devotion.

Gabe lifted Dena into his arms and carried her across the room to the little cot he'd slept on the last seven nights. Groggily she clung to his neck and eyed the narrow folding bed. "I don't know about this, Gabe. That thing's kinda puny, and we're not."

"Can it be any worse than that pool chaise last night?" he asked as he lowered her onto the rumpled bedcovers. Then he could only stare. "Do you have the slightest inkling how damn sexy you look lying there?"

"Yeah." The glass beads of her necklace clinked as she stretched luxuriously. "I do. Come here," she said, with outstretched arms.

Gabe had had a few more side dishes in mind before they got to the main course, but he now found himself helpless to resist Dena's summons, or the frank carnality of her gaze as she watched him obey.

There wasn't room on the cot for him to lie by her side, but that wasn't where he wanted to be anyway. He mounted her, and she opened to him. Her breathing quickened as the rampant tip of his penis prodded her. Steadily he pressed into her slick heat, listening to her soft little gasps, drinking in her wonder-struck smile.

They made slow, sweet love while the sun climbed into the skylight directly overhead. Dena's eyes were impossibly green in the dazzling sunlight. Damp tendrils of hair clung to her brow. In time, slow and sweet gave way to fast and fervid, and Gabe grappled for purchase on the flimsy cot, riding Dena hard as she wrapped herself around him and rose to meet each hammering thrust.

Her eyes flew open and her mouth parted as if in delighted surprise. A quick study, Gabe had learned to interpret that particular look several hours earlier, somewhere between the pool chaise and the fancy shower. *I'm there,* that look said. *I'm there right now!*

"I'm with you, love," he whispered hoarsely, shuddering with his climax, pouring himself into her. *I'm with you as long as you'll have me.*

14

"YOU KNOW WHAT YOU NEED to make this apartment a home?" Dena asked. She sat cross-legged in the corner of the sage-green leather sofa in Gabe's den, watching him mix two black Russians at the polished-teak wet bar. He'd changed into jeans after work, but still wore his white dress shirt, untucked and wrinkled at the bottom, with the sleeves rolled up and the collar open. He was barefoot.

"No, but I'm sure you'll tell me."

"Hey, take it easy with that vodka! You trying to get me drunk?"

"Now, why would I need to get you drunk?" He crossed to the sofa and handed her a glass. "I've already taken advantage of you more ways than I knew existed."

"Funny, I thought it was the other way around." She took a sip of the sweet and fiery coffee-flavored concoction and set it on the thick, triangular slab of glass that topped the cocktail table, an authentic Noguchi piece from the 1940s.

Dena had visited Gabe at his Connecticut apartment regularly during the eight weeks since the class reunion, and the place never ceased to amaze her. The original art by people like Calder and Miró. The exquisite, one-of-a-kind furnishings. The state-of-the-art kitchen and entertainment center.

The king-size bed with Irish linen sheets that almost never got a chance to cool down.

Gabe often visited Dena at her home in West Orange, New Jersey, of course. But her home was just that, a comfortable middle-class home, whereas Gabe's apartment was a pristine masterpiece of professional decorating expertise.

Perhaps that was why he never seemed to really let down his hair here, on his own turf, the way he did at her place, with its mismatched hand-crocheted afghans and overflowing magazine racks, not to mention the basket of yapping puppies tucked into a corner of the sunflower-yellow kitchen.

He sat next to her and turned her bodily so her legs draped over his knees. "Okay, I'll bite. What do I need?"

"A pet. Something to give this place some warmth."

"It's plenty warm when you're here."

Scorching was more like it. "A pug maybe. Those slimy things just don't cut it," she said, nodding toward his fifty-gallon saltwater aquarium teeming with brightly hued fish.

"Trying to sell me the pick of the litter?"

"It'd be a gift. But you have to take care of it, be around for it. You have to be willing to commit."

He sipped his drink in silence, and Dena knew he was pondering her reference to commitment. They saw each other two or three times a week, either here in Greenwich or, more often, at her place, where she could keep an eye on her "babies," the latest litter of black pugs, now five weeks old.

"Commitment's not a problem for me," he said,

in that careful way she'd come to think of as his lawyer mien.

The subtext came through loud and clear. Gabe wanted her to trust that he'd be there for the long haul, that he was committed to their relationship. She wanted to believe him. Certainly he'd done nothing during the last two months to shake her faith in him. But the simple fact was that she'd spent fifteen years living with the pain of his betrayal, and it wasn't easy to throw off her long-standing resentment and mistrust and open herself to him unreservedly.

She toyed with her glass. "Gabe, I have to ask you something. It's...kind of embarrassing."

He was about to make light of her words, she could tell, but something in her expression must have alerted him, because he sobered. "You don't have to be embarrassed with me. What is it?"

"Well...it's about something that happened back when we were at Ham's—something I overheard actually." She glanced fleetingly at him, and took a deep breath. "I didn't mean to eavesdrop. I guess I was just in the right place at the right time. Or the wrong place, depending on your perspective."

"Does this have anything to do with Andrea?"

"No," she said quickly. Andrea was firmly "out of the equation," to use her own phrase. "It's about your parents."

He frowned. "My parents?"

"Your mother actually. I was leaving the house and heard you on the phone with her, and I guess I kind of just stood there and listened."

"Oh." He shrugged. "Hope you weren't too bored."

"Apparently she asked who was staying out at Ham's, and you said some of the people you went to school with. No one special, you said."

She left that hanging there and watched comprehension dawn. For a long moment the glib man of law was at a loss for words.

"I know what you'll say," she continued. "That it doesn't really mean anything. That it's just…one of those things people say." She sighed, wishing she hadn't brought it up.

"It does mean something to you, though," Gabe said gently, wiggling her big toe, encased in a slouchy pumpkin-colored sock. "Don't pretend it doesn't. This has bothered you for weeks."

"It hasn't bothered me."

"That's a crock." He tilted his head, studying her. "I thought I'd seen the last of the old Dena who hid her true feelings and didn't stand up for herself."

She huffed indignantly. "Okay. It's a crock. It bothered the hell out of me. It still does." She sat up straight. "No one special? Gabe, I dated you for nearly a year back in high school! I knew your family, for crying out loud. I was pretty darn 'special' to them at the time, as I recall—the janitor's daughter who had designs on their precious little boy. I thought your mother was going to put her head in the oven over me."

She leaned forward and poked him in the chest. "Do you know I once overheard her telling one of her garden-club cronies that my father was in academic systems maintenance? I was special enough to lie about back then, but I'm not special enough for you to even mention now!"

"Are you finished?"

She stared at him, breathing hard. "Yes." She flopped back against the corner of the couch. "That felt good."

"I'm so pleased. Dena, I don't expect you to necessarily believe this, but the reason I didn't tell them about you is because you *are* so special to me."

She folded her arms and waited, as if to say, *I'm listening*.

He stroked her leg, encased in snug gray leggings printed all over with leaves in autumn colors. "If I'd mentioned you to Mother, I'd have had to listen to all sorts of nonsense from her, the same kind of crap we had to put up with fifteen years ago when we had no choice. Frankly, I opted for the path of least resistance. I do that a lot with her and Dad. It helps keep the peace. Believe me." He closed his hands around Dena's toes and wiggled them all. "It was no reflection on you. You know how I feel about you."

His expression was affable, unconcerned, as if it were impossible to find fault with his logic. He leaned toward her for a kiss. She gently pushed him away.

"You've been seeing me for two months," she said. "Exclusively, I assume."

"You know there's no one else!"

"Can I also assume you still haven't told your folks about us?"

He didn't answer—which, of course, was an answer in itself.

"Oh, Gabe." Dena swung her legs to the floor. "I don't believe this."

"Dena—"

"I do not believe this!" She came to her feet.

So did he. "I told you why—"

"When were you planning on mentioning me?" The answer bopped her on the head like a cartoon anvil. "Unless you weren't. I'm sure you don't tell your folks about every woman who drifts in and out of your life."

"You're not going to drift anywhere if I can help it. You know that."

"I don't know that, Gabe. I know what you say, but..." She turned away.

"Actions speak louder than words, is that it?" he asked.

"No. Yes. Oh, hell."

He came up behind her. She welcomed the pressure of his arms around her waist, the heat of his big, hard body against her back, the familiar scents of shaving soap and laundry starch that had become practically an aphrodisiac for her.

Gabe's huge fish tank dominated her field of vision. It glowed blue-green, reminding her of that night in Ham's hot tub. Their relationship had continued to blossom since then, but it seemed to Dena that the closer they became, the more she was plagued by doubts and uncertainty. He'd told her he loved her on many occasions, but she had yet to reciprocate.

"Dena, don't you remember how strained it was between you and my parents? They scared you to death."

She sent him a quelling look over her shoulder. "I'm not the same scaredy-cat. You know that."

"That's not the point." His arms tightened

around her. "Why give them a chance to sink their fangs in again?"

She said softly, "Trying to protect me from the big bad snobs, Gabe? I seem to recall that already led to disaster once." It was part of the reason he'd asked Andrea to that country-club reception fifteen years ago.

"Dena, you have to trust me on this. I know my parents better than you do. Even if you're willing to put up with that aggravation again, I'm not." He hesitated. "This isn't just about them, is it?"

She turned to face him. "You wonder why I can't just throw myself into this relationship, with no reservations. It's clear to me I have temporary status in your life. This business with your folks is an indicator of where I stand with you."

Sighing, he scrubbed the back of his neck. "So that's what I have to do to demonstrate my commitment? Open us both up to the kind of meddlesome crap that used to make you practically ill? Or is your memory that selective? I recall more than one occasion when my father reduced you to tears, just from his sheer overwhelming presence."

He was right. Dena would be so tense during her visits to Gabe's home, so wound up from her icily polite interactions with his parents, that on a couple of occasions she'd barely made it out of their opulent house before bursting into tears. And the worst part was, she'd known Lucien and Cynthia Moreau were well aware of how cowed she was, how out of her depth.

"Gabe, your parents are a very big part of your life," Dena said. "You work with your father—you're his partner, for heaven's sake! You've abdi-

cated responsibility for your home to your mother."
She gestured at their sumptuously appointed surroundings. "Her decorator designed it, her handpicked three-man cleaning staff comes in twice a week—the easiest money anyone ever made, by the way. I mean, I've never seen a cookie crumb here, or so much as a tilted picture frame. You live in a damn mausoleum!"

"What's your point?" he groused.

"Only that you're still very much influenced by your folks, very much attached to the way of life you grew up with."

"Wait. Is this the same woman who told me how much we've both changed? That we're not the same people we used to be?" He spread his arms. "So I enjoy my career, and the trappings of success. So what? Are you trying to claim we're still worlds apart? Is that it? Because I hate to break the news to you, love, but you kind of closed the distance between us around the time you made your first million."

"It's not about money. It's a class thing. I could be as rich as Trump and your family would never consider me one of them."

"And if they wouldn't, then I wouldn't, right?" He threw up his hands in frustration. "I'm offering you all of me—my love, my future, *our* future. Everything that's within my power to give. And I get the feeling you're not even meeting me halfway."

Dena hugged herself, grappling with her deep-rooted insecurities. She couldn't refute what Gabe was saying. Of the two of them, she was the one who'd held back a part of herself.

His expression softened. He held her lightly. "I

understand," he whispered. "I do. If you're having trouble meeting me halfway, it's my own damn fault."

She started to shake her head.

"It is," he said. "I never denied that. I'll try to be patient, love."

"Oh, Gabe…" She melted against him, rested her head on his shoulder. "I don't want to feel this way. It isn't fair to you. It's not right of me to enter into this relationship making you feel like you have to prove yourself, or make something up to me." She raised her head and looked into his whiskey-colored eyes. "I believe in you. If I didn't, I wouldn't be here. I need you to know that."

"I know it." He touched his lips to hers. "Just try to remember we're starting fresh. It'll work out."

Her smile was tremulous. "Don't say that. It's what we always used to tell each other. 'It'll work out.' Let's just concentrate on the starting-fresh part."

He kissed her again, lingeringly, plucking gently at her lips. "You taste like Kahlúa."

"Mmm…so do you."

"See? A match made in heaven." He deepened the kiss as his hands followed the curve of her back down to her hips and the hem of her burnt-orange satin T-shirt. "You know what I've been thinking about all day?"

"Case law? Jury selection? Torts? What are torts anyway?"

"A kind of dessert. I've been thinking about to-night, and seeing you naked in my bed."

"Good gracious, sir, are you propositioning me?"

"Here's the proposition." Gabe whispered in her

ear, and her response to his first carnal suggestion was to laugh and pull away. He held her still and made her listen to the protracted list of everything he intended to do to her.

"Tell me," she asked, as heat seared her cheeks, "did you get any work done today, thinking up all this stuff?"

"Not a lot, no." He slipped his hands under her satin T-shirt. She began slowly undoing the buttons of his shirt.

"I love weeknights," she said. "I love these dress shirts on you. You look so businesslike, so buttoned up, but so...I don't know...*virile* at the same time with the top open and that sexy chest hair peeking out." She nuzzled the gaping V, gorging her senses on the intoxicating essence of him.

"I changed my mind," he said, backing her toward the sofa. "About getting you into bed. Here is just fine."

His erection nudged her through their clothing. Her body answered with a surge of heat, deep and low. Yes, here was just fine. The sofa had definite possibilities. So did the chairs, the carpet, and the coffee table, for that matter.

"This one's a giveaway." Gabe's hands, still under her shirt, fondled her bra. It had become a game with them, his trying to identify which scandalous brassiere she was wearing, by feel. He always approached the task with scientific thoroughness, taking his time, examining every seam, every bit of trim, loving stroking the cups, carefully gauging cleavage depth and the degree of lift and separation.

Dena had promised him a very special reward if

he ever got it right. He had yet to accomplish that feat, thanks to her vast collection of sexy underthings.

"The black one," he pronounced, and began to pull the shirt up.

She stayed his hand. "*Which* black one?"

"The satin. With the crossed cords in front and that kind of halter thing going on at the shoulders."

"Racer style."

"Whatever. You know the one I mean. I'm right, aren't I?"

She lifted an eyebrow. "And you're sure it's black."

He began to answer.

"Think carefully now."

Gabe's eyes narrowed. She sensed his detail-oriented lawyer's brain sorting through the possibilities. When he spoke, his voice rang with authority. "It's black. Now let's see it."

Dena whipped off the top and displayed her black satin bra. Racer style with crossed cords in front.

Gabe gasped in stunned delight. "I was right!"

She wiped away an imaginary tear. "Gosh, I'm just so darn proud of you."

"What do I get? What's my prize?"

"How about a nice fruit basket?"

"Think again." He propelled them both onto the sofa. His weight pressed her into the soft cushions. He kissed her throat, once, twice. She sighed and reached under his shirt, kneaded his wide back, hot and solid under her hands.

Gabe groped under her back for the bra's hook-and-eye closure.

The phone rang. She jumped. He cursed.

"The machine'll get it," he murmured.

"I'm not in," his recorded voice said. "You know what to do."

The instant Dena heard Wendy Chow's frazzled voice, she shot up off the sofa, shoving Gabe onto the floor. No one on her payroll would bother her here if it weren't urgent.

"I'm trying to get Dena Devlin," Wendy was saying. "We've got a situation here—"

Dena snatched up the phone. "Wendy. What's up?" As she listened to the manager of her newest pet resort describe the problem, she looked at Gabe, lounging on the sofa in his faded jeans and half-open white dress shirt. So close and yet so far.

She sent him an apologetic look. He answered with a wistful smile. The bad news was that she had to leave, which Gabe had obviously figured out. The good news was that this was one man who didn't need to be told that there were times when business came first.

Dena reassured Wendy and hung up the phone. She stood over Gabe with her hands on her hips, in her autumn-leaf leggings and her black Satin Fantasy bra. "Put your shoes on. We've got a reservation at the Xanadu."

15

THE XANADU PET RESORT was located in a charming old brick building in Litchfield that had once been a hotel for human beings. Gabe perused the lobby as Dena met with the manager, a young Asian woman named Wendy Chow, in Wendy's office. The lobby floor was pink marble, the check-in counter gleaming brass and burled wood. Over the counter hung an enormous, gilt-framed oil portrait of a black pug standing proudly against an autumn landscape. It appeared to have been painted in the last century. Gabe had to chuckle. He wasn't the only one with an eye for antique pugs.

On the way there Dena had explained the problem. While every Xanadu resort offered oversize, dormitory-style dog runs, the most sought-after accommodations were the individual apartments. Staff members lived in these apartments, sharing them with a guest dog or cat.

Brenna Rose, a newspaper heiress and an important client of Xanadu, had booked such an apartment for her two poodles. Unfortunately the young man who occupied it, a college student named Mario Messina, had been called away to Naples on a family emergency. Mrs. Rose would be back from her weeklong trip to California tomorrow, but that still left one night that had to be covered.

It was Friday night of the Columbus Day long weekend, prime travel time. All the Xanadu resorts were booked solid, and Wendy had been unable to locate a reliable, trained replacement to fill in. Since Dena was staying close by at Gabe's, the honors had fallen to her.

And to Gabe. Not a dog person by nature, he still wasn't sure how he was going to manage sharing an apartment with a couple of poodles, of all things. German shepherds, he could deal with. He'd even take a pair of Dobermans. A man's dog. But *poodles?*

"Okay, we're set." Dena bustled out of Wendy's office, snatched their sack of Chinese take-out food off the counter and started up the curving, plushly carpeted staircase. She stopped halfway up and sent him a look of studied patience. "You can't sleep in the lobby, Gabe."

Sighing, he lifted their overnight bags and followed behind her. "This ought to tell you how much I love you."

"Stop grumbling. You didn't have to come along." She started down the hallway on the second floor, decorated with an Oriental runner, old-fashioned wall sconces and the ubiquitous antique portraits of dogs and cats.

"We don't get enough time together," Gabe said. "I wasn't going to give up a night with you just because it means sharing you with...poodles."

She smirked at him as she unlocked the door of apartment number seven. Vigorous barking greeted their arrival, a deep man's-dog bark and a yippy little step-on-me-dog bark. The animals bounded toward them as Gabe shut the door. He was surprised. He'd expected a couple of pathetic specimens with pink-dyed fur clipped like topiary hedges, complete with pom-pom tails and hair bows.

One of these dogs was a big fellow—a standard poodle, Dena explained, and a large one at that—with floppy ears and a curly apricot coat trimmed to a uniform thickness. He had to admit it was an attractive animal, even if it wasn't necessarily what he'd call a man's dog. The other one was a toy poodle, a tiny white ball of fuzz, blessedly free of pompoms, that had Dena squealing with delight and scooping it up into her arms.

"Aren't you just the sweetest thing!" she exclaimed as she let the little beast *lick her face!*

Gabe wrinkled his nose. "I hope you're not expecting me to kiss you after that."

"Pay no attention to the mean man," she told the creature as she nuzzled and stroked it. "He's a *lawyer*," she stage-whispered into its furry ear. "Need I say more? Now, which one are you? Susie or Shaynie?"

The big standard poodle responded enthusiastically to the second name, so there was one mystery solved. They were both girl dogs, then. *Outnumbered*, Gabe thought. Naturally.

Shaynie appeared overly interested in the bag of Chinese food. Dena moved it into the kitchen, then knelt and quickly made friends with the big dog, speaking to her in a high, friendly voice, letting her sniff her hands and offering doggie yummies from her shoulder bag.

"You got anything in there for me?" Gabe asked. "Like a handful of Valium?"

"The mean man is trying to be funny," she told Shaynie. "Sad, isn't it?"

"I'll move our bags," he grumbled, scoping the place out and quickly locating the bedroom. It was a cozy, utilitarian apartment, ideal for a single student like the young man who lived here. More than ideal for pampered mutts like Susie and Shaynie.

When he reentered the living room, Dena was flipping through papers on a clipboard. "Okay, let's see what we have here. Shaynie likes to watch NASCAR racing on ESPN, and usually falls asleep in the middle of it. Susie stays up for *I Love Lucy* reruns on Nickelodeon." She checked her watch.

"Oh, please," Gabe said. "Tell me the dogs don't get to pick the TV shows."

"The usual choice is the Discovery Channel, with the Food Network running a close second. But these gals don't seem to run with the pack. So to speak. Oh, and they both like Lite FM," she said, consulting the notes, "although we are warned that Shaynie likes to howl along to Sting's 'Fields of Gold.'" She rubbed the big dog's head. "I'm with you, Shaynie. That's just the most romantic song."

"Okay, one question," Gabe said. "Where do they sleep?"

Dena grinned. "That's like asking where a thousand-pound lion sleeps." She spread her arms. "Wherever they want to."

Gabe pointed toward the bedroom. "The bed's ours, though, right? I mean, these are *dogs*. They sleep on, like, dog beds or something." He looked around. No dog beds in sight.

She grabbed two leashes off a hook by the door.

"Are you going to be this anxious and upset all night?"

"I'm not anxious and upset, I just want to know— What are you doing?"

"Taking these ladies outside for a few minutes. Come along and keep us company."

He did, and found himself impressed by the resort's huge yard, about a half acre, meticulously landscaped. Dena explained that all canine guests were brought outside for play and exercise several times a day.

When they returned to the apartment, she tuned in to NASCAR racing on the TV, but thankfully kept the volume low. Shaynie planted herself in front of the set, while Susie seemed more interested in Dena and Gabe's dinner preparations as they set their take-out feast on the small table in the L-shaped dining alcove.

Dena settled herself in her chair across from Gabe. "I know you've already eaten," she told the dog. "General Tso's Chicken isn't what your little tummy needs." She lifted a rawhide chew toy from the carpet and tossed it into the living room. Susie watched it land and turned back to stare at the General Tso's Chicken.

"I just know I'm going to step on that hair ball," Gabe muttered as he dug in to his pork lo mein. "It's always underfoot."

As if Susie knew he was talking about her, she trotted to his side and sat staring up at him, tracking his every movement with her dark little eyes. He lifted a few strands of lo mein with his chopsticks and held them over her head.

"Don't you dare!" Dena scolded.

"What's the worst that can happen?"

"That *you'll* be up with her all night. In the yard."

Gabe popped the lo mein into his own mouth. Susie scooted closer still, licking her chops.

Eventually the toy poodle lost interest and went into the living room to harass Shaynie, who had begun to doze. Susie leaped on the much larger animal and bit her tail. Shaynie came instantly awake, snarling and snapping, batting at the tiny dog and trying to chomp it.

"Aren't you going to stop them?" Gabe demanded.

Dena spared them only a glance. "They're just playing."

The two animals didn't look like they were playing. Susie, the instigator, fought like a demon, biting the big dog every chance she got. Shaynie had the obvious advantage and easily immobilized Susie, closing her huge jaws over the furry little head.

Gabe was out of his seat like a shot. "Shaynie! Stop that! Dena, she's going to kill it!"

"If Shaynie wanted to kill Susie, that little devil would've been lunch a long time ago. Mind if I finish the lo mein?"

Gabe didn't answer, too distracted by the sight of Susie, having been released with her cranium intact, pouncing on Shaynie yet again. Gabe would have thought she'd learned her lesson. Once more the big dog threatened to devour the little one.

"You see?" Dena said. "Playing."

Gabe dropped into his chair and picked up his chopsticks. "Yeah," he griped, "but where are they going to sleep?"

This man needed a real pet, Dena thought. Something warm-blooded, with fur and a personality. Something he wouldn't mind curling up with on a chilly night. Those exotic fish of his were closer to kinetic sculpture than pets.

Not for the first time, she thought of how it would be to share her big, eclectic house with Gabe. She thought of how much he enjoyed playing with her spirited puppies, how delicious he looked sprawled on her queen-size sleigh bed, bathed in early morning sunlight slanting through the dormer window. With the white bedsheets twisted around his naked body and his light brown hair in disarray and his jaw rough with beard stubble, he looked more like some kind of old-west desperado, or an outlaw biker perhaps, than a partner in one of Wall Street's most prestigious law firms.

"What are you thinking?" Gabe asked. "What put that dreamy expression on your face?"

"I'm thinking how irresistible you look in my bed."

His whiskey eyes darkened to maple syrup. He glanced at the door to the bedroom. "What do you say we leave the little darlings to their bloodbath and turn in early?"

The "bloodbath" had wound down. The little darlings were now tussling over a squeaky rubber dog bone.

"I wish we could," Dena said, as they started clearing the white cardboard take-out containers off the table. "But we really have to spend a little quality time with these guys."

Gabe muttered something under his breath, but he didn't argue.

Two hours later, Shaynie was snoring on the love

seat. Gabe lounged in an armchair in front of the television, absently stroking the fluffy little dog curled up in his lap, both absorbed in Lucy and Ethel's latest harebrained scheme.

Dena got ready for bed and padded back out to the living room wearing a short white silk robe covered in hot pink kissy lips. On-screen, an exasperated Ricky scolded, "Looo-ceeee…" Gabe snorted. Susie's ear pricked.

"I hate to break this up," Dena said, "but I thought you were ready to turn in."

Gabe did a classic double take worthy of Ricky Ricardo, eyeing Dena's state of dishabille. "I'm ready," he said, and lost no time turning over the armchair to the tiny poodle.

Dena had turned down the covers on the double platform bed. The only light came from several short votive candles in glass holders, which she'd arranged on the nightstands. Gabe followed her into the bedroom, took one look at her handiwork and kicked the door shut. He unfastened the buttons of his white shirt with lightning speed and tossed it in a corner, even as he kicked off his shoes.

"You're in a hurry," Dena laughed.

He advanced on her where she stood near the bed. Flickering candlelight accentuated the sinewy terrain of his bare torso. "We were interrupted back at my place," he said, as his fingers went to the fly of his jeans. He popped the brass button free. "Now, where were we exactly?"

"On the sofa in your den." She stroked her hands up his warm chest. "You were intent on collecting your prize, as I recall."

"My prize? Oh yeah." His hands came up to fondle her breasts through the silk robe. His brow knitted. "What are you wearing under this?"

He started to pull the robe open. Dena playfully swatted his hands away and shoved him so he fell onto the bed.

"Patience." She knelt on the mattress, straddling him. "Some things are worth waiting for."

He folded his arms under his head. "So what's my prize?" he asked. "Don't keep me in suspense any longer."

"I'll keep you in suspense as long as I feel like it."

His smiling eyes glittered in the warm candlelight. "Ooh, tough lady."

"That's right." Dena slid onto the floor, where she knelt between his legs. Lightly she touched the distended front of his jeans. His breathing picked up speed; he watched her intently. She grasped the zipper pull and slowly worked it down his fly until the denim gaped open, revealing white briefs stretched taut.

Dena bent over him and pressed her lips to the straining fabric. Gabe's breath left him in a rush. He caressed her hair, wordlessly encouraging her. Not that Dena needed any encouragement. She hooked her fingers in the waistband of his jeans to pull them off.

Gabe jerked up with a strangled cry, holding his pants closed. Dena whipped around to see what had alarmed him, and came face-to-face with Shaynie, not a foot away. Shaynie's tail wagged. Hot dog breath fanned Dena's face.

The raw curses erupting from Gabe had Dena biting her lip, trying not to laugh. Shaynie climbed onto the bed and got herself settled.

"How the hell did that thing get in here!" he cried, zipping up. "I closed the damn door!"

"Some dogs are very clever," she said, scratching the big poodle behind the ears. "They can open doors. Or maybe it didn't latch."

Gabe stalked to the door and examined it. "There's no lock! How are we supposed to keep them out?"

Dena shrugged. "They're dogs, Gabe. Who cares if they come in?"

"*I* care! I can't...relax and enjoy myself with that thing watching me."

Dena gave up the battle to control her giggles. "I don't think Shaynie has voyeuristic tendencies. I think she just wants company. Isn't that right, girl?"

He pointed a stern finger at the dog. "Her company—" he pointed toward the living room "—is out there. That's where she belongs."

Susie trotted into the bedroom, alerted by the racket, no doubt, wanting in on the excitement. She jumped onto the bed.

"Oh God." Gabe slumped against the wall, defeated.

Dena rose and went over to him. She slid her arms around his waist and kissed his throat.

Gabe's hands closed over her shoulders, as if to push her away. His voice was tight. "They're watching us."

"Mmm-hmm." She trailed her lips to his shoulder and lightly nipped him. Her hands slipped down to his buttocks.

"Never knew you were an exhibitionist."

"Let's go into the other room." She licked his shoulder.

"They'll just follow us," he moaned. "It's no use. We're going to have to wait till we get back home."

"I can't believe you're letting a couple of dumb beasts dictate your love life."

He brightened. "We can lock ourselves in the bathroom."

"I'm sorry, I am not going to make love in the john just because you're too priggish to—"

"Priggish? You call *me* priggish?"

Dena crossed to the bed and blew out all the candles on the nightstands. She turned on a gooseneck reading lamp so the dogs wouldn't be left in the dark, then grabbed Gabe's arm and pulled him out of the room. She closed the door to the bedroom, making sure the latch caught. Gabe stared balefully at the door.

"This looks like a very comfortable sofa," she said, turning off lights and the TV, leaving on only one small table lamp.

He sighed. "I don't think this is going to work, Dena. I'm just too tense."

"I thought you wanted to collect your prize."

The look on his face said he'd forgotten about the prize. "Well, you can give it to me when we're home."

"I think I'll give it to you now."

"Dena—"

His words died when she opened her robe and let it fall to the carpet. She wore a baby-blue leather corset laced tightly up the back. The scandalous garment pushed her breasts to the stratosphere, exposing her nipples. Matching blue lace thong panties completed the outfit.

Dena stroked her hands lovingly over the buttery

soft leather. "I thought of you when I found this. Do you like it?"

Gabe's wry chuckle was answer enough. "Turn around," he said, and she did. "Oh, Dena..."

She heard him come up behind her, felt his warm breath on her shoulders, the feathery touch of his fingers skipping down the crisscrossed lacing.

He said, "How did you get this on by yourself?"

"Where there's a will there's a way." She glanced over her shoulder. Had she ever seen him look this hungry? "I wanted to surprise you."

"Love, if I live to be a hundred, you'll never stop surprising me."

Dena ignored the casual reference to their shared future. If truth be told, she kind of liked the idea of surprising this man for a few more decades.

Gabe's hands glided around her cinched waist and up her rib cage. He molded the shape of her uplifted breasts, plucked the stiff nipples. She shivered and leaned back into him. He kissed her bare shoulder.

"I love the way you smell," he said, kissing a trail to her throat. "I've always loved the way you smell. For fifteen years I'd wake up trying to hold on to the scent of you, fading with my dreams."

He turned her around, almost roughly, and crushed her to him, capturing her mouth in a hard kiss. His urgency was more than physical, Dena knew, it was a primitive drive, an instinct to bind her to him, body and soul.

Gabe raised his head and briefly glanced toward the sofa, before reality intruded. He speared the closed door of the bedroom with a malignant glare, as if expecting Shaynie to come charging out any second snapping photographs.

"We'll be very quiet so they don't get excited," Dena said soothingly, urging him toward the sofa and pushing him until he sat. "They're probably asleep already." She knelt in front of him.

"Dena..." he said as she unzipped his jeans for the second time that evening. "Love, I just don't think I can—" He broke off abruptly.

"Oh, I think you can," she said as she liberated an erection that could only be called majestic. "I'd say there's no doubt on that score."

He sagged against the sofa as she caressed him, his groans interspersed with dark mutterings about the damn dogs.

Dena figured if she wasn't woman enough to make him forget about the damn dogs, she may as well hang up her corset. She peeled off his jeans and briefs, and moved between his thighs. His hot gaze drank in her corseted form as she stroked and fondled him. She lowered her head, and the air left his lungs in a rush.

For the next few minutes she was reasonably certain the damn dogs were the furthest thing from his mind. His long, strong fingers splayed over her scalp, holding her to him, directing the rhythm. His hoarse sighs filled her ears as she loved him with her mouth. He murmured words of endearment, words of encouragement.

Finally he made her stop. He was close, she knew. She objected, wanted to pleasure him fully, but already he was pulling her onto his lap, stripping off her panties.

"I need you," he growled. "I need to be inside

you." Digging his fingers into her hips, he drove up into her in one forceful thrust.

The pleasure was sharp and sudden, almost brutal in intensity. Dena cried out. She clung to him, her anchor, as physical sensation threatened to overwhelm her.

Gabe felt it, too. One look at his face and she knew he was as helplessly consumed by it as she. He lifted and lowered her, filling her, stretching her, propelling her ever closer to the shimmering brink of release.

"Oh, love…" he groaned, grimacing with the effort to delay his own orgasm, for her sake.

"Now," she panted. "Now, Gabe. Now!"

His climax overtook him, every muscle and tendon straining as he bucked fiercely under her, into her. His hammering finish pushed her over the brink. Dena smiled, startled, as she always was, by the simple perfection of it. And then she lost herself to the awesome pumping energy, safe in the sanctuary of Gabe's arms.

16

"I WENT SHOPPING TODAY," Dena called, from her bedroom upstairs.

"What a shock," Gabe said dryly. His ladylove was no stranger to power-shopping. If she ever cut up her credit cards, the department stores would hang black crape.

He sat cross-legged on the floor of her living room, playing with her three black pug puppies, now two months old and recently weaned. Dena had renewed her offer of the pick of the litter. Gabe was tempted to accept, but the idea of removing one of these lively little dogs from this warm, delightfully chaotic home and installing it in his "mausoleum" of an apartment just didn't sit right with him.

The puppies' mother, Hermione, kept watch from the hearth rug where she lay curled before the low fire. It was only mid-October, but a cold snap had moved in, prompting Gabe to trek out to the woodpile Dena kept at the rear of her yard for some kindling and a couple of logs.

The puppies ganged up on him, vying for the squeaky ball he teased them with, their curled tails wagging. He raised his voice to be heard over their yapping. "What did you buy?"

"A dress. For the party."

"You have a closet full of dresses. You didn't have to buy a new one. Oh, silly me. Look who I'm talking to."

Gabe had tried not to dwell too much on the party they were to attend that evening. If Dena was anxious, she hid it well. His law firm, Moreau Pittman, was holding a party celebrating its thirtieth anniversary—at the Briarfield Country Club, the location not only of Gabe and Dena's fateful high-school reunion three months ago, but the legendary scene of the crime that had caused their breakup two months before graduation.

This affair was eerily similar to that long-ago reception, except that it was even more formal, a black-tie dinner dance. Gabe had invited Dena as soon as he'd found out about it. He didn't want to think of tonight as a watershed point in their relationship, but it was hard not to.

He'd made progress the past few weeks, getting her to let down her guard and open herself to him and to what they had together. Still, he sensed an underlying reserve, nurtured, no doubt, by ugly memories of her visits to Château Moreau, her pet name for his parents' ostentatious home.

And tonight she'd have to face them again.

"Do you want to see the dress?" she called, and Gabe detected a soupçon of nervous anticipation.

"Of course!" he said.

She descended the staircase. He stared. When he could speak, he said, "Who are you, and what have you done with Dena?"

She chuckled nervously and patted her hair, which she'd swept away from her face into a sleek knot at her nape. How she'd gotten the curls to lie flat was beyond him.

The gown she'd chosen was a sleeveless, ankle-length column of matte navy silk, with a small key-hole opening in the high neckline. The epitome of understated elegance, it was exquisitely con-structed and obviously expensive. Unlike every other dress Dena owned, this one skimmed her en-ticing curves without adhering to them—flattering but far from suggestive. Her only jewelry was a pair of small pearl-and-diamond drop earrings that he'd never seen before.

Gabe came to his feet as Dena performed a slow pirouette. The gown drifted around her statuesque form with a sigh. The puppies fell over themselves chasing the swirling hem.

She took a deep breath. "What do you think?"

"You look...perfect. Absolutely perfect for this kind of affair."

She sighed in relief, and gave her new do another pat.

"Now go change," he said.

She blinked. "What?"

"I appreciate the effort, but, Dena, this isn't you."

"Gabe, don't be ridiculous. This outfit is perfect. You just said so."

"You look like Princess Grace, done up like this. What happened to you and Marilyn Monroe, sepa-rated at birth?"

She glowered. "Marilyn never had to go to a black-tie affair for Moreau Pittman."

"You don't have to wear a costume, pretend to be someone you aren't. I'd never ask that of you."

Her eyes flashed with anger. "You've got a lot of

nerve. Fifteen years ago you wouldn't even *take* me to something like this because I wasn't—" She clamped her lips shut. Clearly she hadn't wanted to bring that up.

He stroked her bare arms. "I'm so proud of you, love. And I'm going to be so damn proud to walk into that ballroom with you on my arm. You. The woman I love." He smiled. "Grace Kelly's not my type."

"Whatever happened to the path of least resistance?"

"Evasion techniques only work up to a certain point. Then you've got to lace up the gloves."

She grimaced. "You haven't told your folks about me yet, have you?"

They hadn't discussed it since that night four weeks earlier. It seemed they'd both made a conscious decision to keep the peace by avoiding the issue. It could no longer be avoided.

"It's better this way," Gabe said. "When they meet you again tonight, you'll win them over. I know you will."

"So that's the strategy, huh?" she asked, with a droll expression. "Blindside them with me at this ritzy affair where they can't make a fuss?"

"Gosh, the idea never even occurred to me."

"Yeah, right. Gabe, this is going to be a disaster."

"It'll only be a disaster if you try to remake yourself into what you think is expected."

"People do alter their appearance when they attend certain functions, you know. Even me. It's called dressing appropriately."

"I'm not saying you have to wear your most outrageous outfit tonight, Dena. I'm just saying I want you to be you. And what would be the point of a drastic transformation anyway? You couldn't keep it up forever."

That final word buzzed between them like static. *Forever.* Her eyes sought his. He wasn't sure what he read in them. Perhaps he didn't want to know. Yet he couldn't help adding, "Forever, Dena. If I have anything to say about it."

Dena's lips trembled. Her eyes misted. "I do love you, Gabe."

His chest swelled. He pulled her to him, hard.

"I love you so much," she murmured into his shoulder, her voice watery. "I don't know why it took me so long to say it."

"I know why. And I think you do, too." She'd been guarding her heart, which he'd broken once. That she trusted him with it now filled him with awe. Smiling, he kissed her temple. "I kind of knew you were sweet on me, but it sure is nice to hear the words."

THE BALLROOM of the Briarfield Country Club was done up even swankier than the only other time Dena had seen it, three months earlier at the class reunion. Even from the doorway she recognized the glittering Christofle silver and Baccarat crystal that had been laid on snowy white damask tablecloths. Striking floral centerpieces perfumed the air. Enormous logs burned in the two oversize carved-oak fireplaces. The twenty-piece band set up on a stage near the parquet dance floor did credit to the familiar old standard they were playing.

But the most conspicuous difference between the reunion and this extravagant affair was the guests themselves, mingling over beluga caviar and imported champagne. Never in her life had Dena seen so many tuxedos in one place; the men looked like they'd been stamped out by a cookie cutter. The women were more colorful but no less uniform in their designer gowns, heirloom jewelry and over-coiffed hair.

"I may need those tendons someday," Gabe said, and only then did Dena realize how far she'd sunk her burgundy-colored fingernails into the arm of his tuxedo jacket.

"No one has noticed me yet," she said. "We don't have to go through with this."

"If you make a run for it, I swear I'll throw you over my shoulder and carry you in like a sack of potatoes."

He was smiling!

"This isn't funny!" she hissed. "Look at me! Why did you make me change?"

He actually laughed! "As if I could *make* you do anything."

"You were right, Gabe," she moaned. "That other dress was perfect." She punched his arm.

"You know, if I didn't love you so much, this abuse might really start getting to me. Dena, stop fretting. You look incredible."

"That's what I'm afraid of."

"You know what I mean. You're beautiful, love. More than beautiful, enchanting." The glint in his eyes said he wasn't lying.

"You're hardly impartial," she muttered.

After their earlier conversation, she'd unpinned that Grace Kelly hairdo, shampooed out all the gel and spray and let it dry in fluffy waves around her face while she'd flipped through dresses in her massive walk-in closet. She'd kept coming back to the same gown, one that had been created especially for her by a young friend of hers, an aspiring designer and recent graduate of New York's Fashion Institute of Technology.

As soon as Gabe had seen it on her, he'd cried, "Dena! You're back!"

The gown's first layer was a body-hugging stretch velvet minidress in a rich burgundy color, high-necked with a little stand-up collar of bronze brocade. What the dress lacked in cleavage, it made up for in exposed shoulders, thanks to armholes cut in toward the collar.

Dena often wore this base alone as a short cocktail dress, but tonight she'd added the dramatic, ankle-length overskirt: overlapping, petal-like layers of sheer silk organza in burgundy, dark green and bronze, attached to a wide bronze brocade cummerbund laced snugly around her midriff and dipping to a point in front. Her legs were visible through the filmy organza, right down to her stiletto-heeled burgundy velvet slingbacks.

She only hoped no one noticed her knees shaking.

Gabe reached over to flick a dangling, garnet-encrusted earring. "You look like Cinderella with attitude."

"Is it midnight yet?"

He squeezed her hand. "Just stick with me."

A deep male voice called, "Gabe!"

Dena groaned. Too late to escape. They'd been spotted.

Please don't let it be Lucien Moreau, she thought. *Not yet.*

Her prayers were answered, barely. Gabe introduced her to Robert Pittman, Andrea's father and the firm's other founding partner. He was of medium height, with thinning hair just turning gray at the temples. He had his daughter's silver-gray eyes. Despite the fact that the Pittmans and Moreaus were lifelong best friends, this was the first time Dena had met Andrea's father. Gabe's parents had never invited her to any of their social gatherings during the eleven months she'd dated their son.

Dena offered her hand, chagrined that as calm as she managed to act, her cold, clammy fingers had to give her away. If Pittman noticed, he gave no clue. A waiter approached with an hors d'oeuvre-laden tray. The men helped themselves to lobster-stuffed endive, but she declined. For once, her appetite had deserted her.

Pittman's smile seemed genuine as he said, "Can I assume you're the reason this guy goes around with a sappy grin on his face nowadays?"

Gabe slid his arm around her waist. "So it's that obvious, is it?"

Pittman said, "My paralegal's been giving odds on whether you'll be engaged by the end of the year."

"So where'd you put your money?" Gabe asked.

"On a Christmas wedding."

Dena laughed, charmed despite herself by Andrea's surprisingly affable father. "And without even meeting me! Gabe, just how goofy are you acting around the office?"

Gabe pulled himself up in mock affront. "Not goofy. Besotted."

"Now that I've met this lovely lady you've been keeping under wraps," Pittman said, "I think I'll move my bet up to Thanksgiving."

He met her gaze directly, the corners of his eyes crinkling. Despite any previous expectations, Andrea's father appeared resigned to the fact that his daughter and the son of his closest friend were never going to tie the knot. He seemed genuinely happy for Gabe.

Eager to change the subject, Dena said, "Congratulations, Mr. Pittman. It must be a wonderful feeling to celebrate the thirtieth anniversary of the law firm you helped found."

"Call me Bob. A wonderful feeling? Dena, it's beyond wonderful. It's—well, it's stupendous. And the most stupendous part is knowing that with the next generation at the helm, Moreau Pittman will be around until well into the next millennium. Kind of like a little dose of immortality." He looked fondly at Gabe, who responded with a respectful nod.

And Dena finally got it. As she watched the two men share a silent, heartfelt exchange, she finally comprehended the full extent of Gabe's love for, and devotion to, his work. She'd always assumed his parents had somehow coerced him into the family business, had taken advantage of his sense of duty and dedication to his family. But in that moment she knew in her heart that the firm his father and Bob Pittman had founded thirty years ago was more than a job for Gabe. It was his legacy. And it made him happy.

Bob motioned to someone to join them. "Gwen, come meet the mystery lady."

He introduced Dena to his wife, Gwen Pittman, an attractive woman of about sixty. She, too, was cordial, although she seemed to be trying a little too hard. Dena supposed it was better than the alternative.

"It's very nice to meet you." Mrs. Pittman's brow wrinkled. "Dena Devlin. That name sounds familiar. Didn't you go to high school here in Briarfield, with Gabe and Andrea?"

"Yes, I did. I graduated the same year." Would she remember that Dena had gone steady with her presumptive future son-in-law? Had her daughter or the Moreaus even mentioned her at the time?

Probably not, Dena decided as she watched Andrea's mother try to place her, and fail.

"Do you live in Greenwich now, too?" Mrs. Pittman asked.

"No, New Jersey."

"Well, there are some lovely neighborhoods in New Jersey. I don't believe I know your parents—although, of course, we moved to Larchmont years ago. Were they members?"

It took Dena a moment to realize Mrs. Pittman was referring to the country club. She obviously assumed Gabe would only escort one of the elite to a function like this. His arm tightened fractionally around her waist, his protective instincts clearly aroused.

"No, they didn't belong to the club."

"I seem to recall a Devlin on the board of the local historical society. Could that have been your mother?"

Dena gave the other woman her most engaging smile. "I'm afraid not. My mother was kept busy raising five children and working as an aide at the Briarfield Nursing Home. You might've met my father, though. He was a janitor at the high school."

Mrs. Pittman's brittle smile locked in place with an almost audible click. She appeared at a loss for words.

Not so her husband. "Do they still live in Briarfield?" he asked as he lifted a flute of champagne from a passing waiter's tray and handed it to Dena before taking one for himself.

"No, they retired to Maine two years ago."

Bob's silver eyes lit up. "Does your dad fish?"

"No, but Mom is a champion fly fisherwoman. She says she moved to paradise."

Bob smiled wistfully. "Maine."

Gwen Pittman appeared to have recovered. "Now, don't get Bob started on fishing." She turned to Gabe. "Dear, your father was looking for you a little while ago."

Every muscle in Dena's body tensed. She sipped her champagne, felt the tiny bubbles tickle her tongue.

"Listen, you two have to come over for dinner," Bob said. "Soon."

"Oh yes, that would be lovely," his wife agreed. "Next Sunday?"

Gabe turned to Dena. "How about it, love? Are you free Sunday?" He knew she was free; he was offering her a chance to decline.

"I sure am," Dena said. "Thank you. I'm looking forward to it."

Gabe gave her waist a little squeeze.

Andrea's mother was animated now that she had an opportunity to entertain. "Why don't we plan on seven o'clock. Tell me, Dena, is there anything you don't eat?"

Grinning, she gestured to her hips. "Do I look like there's anything I don't eat?"

Mrs. Pittman reacted with a spontaneous titter, which Dena considered a minor victory. "Now, I know you're just having fun with me. You have a lovely figure, dear." Looking past Dena, she wagged her fingers at someone.

Dena looked over her shoulder and watched Andrea approach, watched the flare of surprise, quickly extinguished, as she noticed Dena. They exchanged vapid greetings and Andrea introduced everyone to her date, Spencer Williams, a senior associate in a midtown law firm. Classically handsome, impeccably groomed and sporting the ubiquitous black tux, Spencer looked like an escapee from Barbie's Dream House: Formal Wear Ken in the flesh.

Andrea wore a sleek navy gown disturbingly similar to the one Dena had modeled for Gabe earlier.

First thing tomorrow, she was taking it back to the store.

Andrea turned to her father. "The D.A.'s office should be getting back to us with—"

Bob held up his palm. "It'll keep till Monday. Tonight we're celebrating. No shop talk."

Gabe said, "I see my parents over there. Let's go catch them while they're still together."

Dena's heart squirmed into her throat. She said her nice-to-meet-yous and set aside her half-full champagne flute. Gabe took her hand and led her across the room. People greeted him along the way, and he made fleeting introductions. Dena responded on autopilot, smiling brightly and saying all the right things, but all she could think about was Lucien and Cynthia Moreau getting ever closer in her peripheral vision.

It was as if she'd been transported back in time. As if she were turning back into the self-conscious, easily intimidated girl she'd once been.

This is ridiculous, she told herself. She had nothing to be nervous about. Gabe loved her, and that was all that mattered. Regardless of how his parents reacted, he'd still love her, because he believed in her.

That thought brought her up short. Gabe did believe in her. He was proud of her. He'd said it often enough, and he was proving it even now. He was right—she'd been holding back a part of herself, fearful, on some gut level, of a repeat of the wrongs and hurts of her youth. But as Gabe strode right up to his parents with her in tow, every last lingering doubt evaporated. She couldn't help smiling at her own foolishness, and that was how the Moreaus first saw her, standing by their son's side, beaming proudly, practically daring them to disapprove.

"Gabriel!" his mother said. "We were wondering where you were. I was just telling Helmut—" She stopped abruptly, staring at Dena. Her husband, too, fixed his gaze on her.

Lucien Moreau was even more imposing than Dena remembered, as tall as his son and powerfully built. His thick, neatly trimmed hair was fully silver now, in dramatic contrast to his deeply suntanned face, the result of a lifelong love of sailboating.

Gabe squeezed her hand. He said, "Mom, Dad, you remember Dena Devlin, I'm sure."

Dena took a deep breath, released her death grip on Gabe and extended her hand. "Mr. and Mrs. Moreau, it's so good to see you again."

Gabe's father was the first to shake her proffered hand, an automatic impulse, no doubt. His mother followed suit.

"My goodness. Dena." Cynthia Moreau's eyes skittered over Dena's distinctive gown. "It has been a long time. Hasn't it, Lucien?"

"Yes," was all he said. His flat stare shifted from Dena to Gabe, where it lingered—accusingly, Dena thought.

For his part, Gabe held his father's gaze for several beats longer than strictly required, before turning away to introduce Dena to the man his parents had been chatting with, an elegant, white-haired gentleman with a cultured German accent. Dena immediately connected this Helmut Danziger to the German-based H. Danziger Corporation, one of the world's leading manufacturers of optical equipment.

Gabe's parents exchanged a brief look. Their indignation was palpable. Dena found herself chewing back a grin. She almost felt sorry for them. After fifteen years, they had to have thought they'd seen the last of their son's lowbrow high-school sweetheart. They must have long since thanked God he'd seen the light and ended the wrongheaded flirtation.

Dena felt like something out of the movie *Poltergeist.*

I'm baa-ack!

And suddenly she was enjoying every minute of it.

17

DENA GAVE Lucien Moreau's arm a friendly pat. "I'll bet you're wondering how Gabe and I hooked up again. We ran into each other back in July at the reunion. Right here at the Briarfield Country Club!"

Lucien turned to address Helmut Danziger.

"So. Mr. Moreau," Dena said, knowing he couldn't ignore a direct question. "How does it feel to be celebrating thirty years?"

Slowly he turned back to her, said blandly, "There are no words for what I'm feeling right now."

"Talk about evasive!" She grinned at Gabe and Danziger. "Isn't that just like a lawyer?"

A ripple of laughter answered her. There was a funny light in Gabe's eye as he watched her. She sensed he was ready to jump in at any moment, had probably planned to do all the talking. For now, though, he seemed content to listen.

She said, "I asked Bob Pittman the same thing. He was a tad more loquacious on the subject."

"You've been talking to Bob?" Cynthia glanced nervously at her husband.

"And Gwen, too. I've been trying to meet everyone here, all the people Gabe works with!" Dena gushed, a sadistic impulse on her part, considering the fact that all the firm's most important clients were in attendance.

One of those clients, of course, was Helmut Danziger. He turned to Dena. "Do you also practice law, Miss Devlin?"

Cynthia quickly interjected, "No, Dena is Gabe's friend."

"A very good friend, yes?" Danziger's smile was warm. "You are not with the firm, then?"

"Nein, Herr Danziger," Dena replied. *"Ich habe verschiedene Hotels für Hunde und Katzen."* I have several hotels for dogs and cats.

Danziger's eyes grew round. *"Ja?"*

Cynthia tugged on Gabe's sleeve. Dena just made out their whispered conversation. "What did she say?" his mother hissed.

"She said she gives dogs tick baths and her father's a janitor."

Cynthia glared at her husband as if to say, *Do something!*

"I believe the first course is being served," Lucien announced, with booming authority. "Shall we find our seats?"

Dena ended up sitting between Gabe and Herr Danziger. Gabe's parents, the Pittmans, Andrea and Formal Wear Ken completed the table. Dena continued to converse in German with the charming Herr Danziger, about everything from the relative merits of German versus Japanese camera optics to his favorite Rottweiler's picky eating habits. Dena had excelled at German in junior high and high school, and had honed her skills on her former employer Frau Buchler while shampooing countless canines at Going to the Dogs.

Gabe's mother seemed to have turned into a picky eater herself this evening. She made a conspicuous effort at lighthearted conversation, while her jittery gaze kept returning to Elly May Clampett and the Very Important Client she was chatting up in a foreign tongue.

Outwardly Gabe's father appeared unaffected by whatever havoc Dena might be wreaking. On those occasions when his penetrating dark brown eyes homed in on her, she had the distinct impression he was sending her a message. Or a warning.

For his part, Gabe smiled serenely and said isn't this some brisk weather we're having.

"I'm afraid I'm being rude," Dena finally said to the table at large. "Doubly rude. Not only have I monopolized Helmut, but I've subjected the poor man to my mediocre German."

"*Nein, nein!*" he objected. "*Ich verstehe Sie sehr gut.* I understand you very well. You are quite fluent, Dena. I have enjoyed our conversation immensely." He turned to Gabe's father. "This is quite a special young lady, Lucien. You must be very proud of her."

"A facility with languages is much to be admired," Lucien said evenly.

"And a facility in matters of commerce even more so, you must agree," Helmut replied. "I am referring, of course, to Dena's business venture."

Gabe's father wasn't so quick with a reply this time. He glanced at Gabe, clearly expecting his son to jump in and provide some hint as to what Helmut was talking about. It would have been awkward for Lucien to admit his ignorance in the face of his client's enthusiasm.

Gabe set down his salad fork. "Personally, I couldn't be more proud of Dena." He seemed inclined to let his folks sweat a bit.

Not so Andrea. "Of course, we're all very impressed." She addressed Helmut, although her words were, of course, meant to enlighten the Moreaus. "Such a clever idea, a fancy pet hotel as an alternative to boarding kennels. And the idea took off! How many Xanadu Pet Resorts are there now, Dena?"

"Six. I'm looking into opening a seventh in Owings Mills, Maryland."

Lucien's expression never changed. Cynthia, however, couldn't conceal her surprise. "Pet hotels?" she asked Dena, wide-eyed. "You mean like with little rooms?"

"The animal lives in an apartment on the premises with one of the staff. We also offer large dog runs, which are more economical, but the apartments are always booked well in advance."

"And no wonder! Do the dogs get to spend time outdoors?" Cynthia asked, shushing her husband when he attempted to redirect the conversation.

"Of course," Dena said, as a waiter removed her salad plate. "All the Xanadu resorts have big yards. And they all offer grooming and obedience training."

"A pet resort! What a brilliant concept!" Cynthia cried. "And long overdue! I feel so terribly guilty every time I take a trip and have to leave my precious babies at the kennel." She seized her husband's arm. "Lucien, isn't this the most wonderful news!"

"Wonderful," Lucien agreed, in a monotone.

"You mean you didn't know about Xanadu?" Helmut asked.

Cynthia drew herself up. "If I'd known, do you think I would have left my precious babies at a *kennel?*"

"What breed are we talking about?" Dena asked.

"Shih Tzu. Two girls, Amber and Topaz. They're little darlings, they really are. I don't know what I'd do without them. Last Easter Lucien and I went to the south of France and I worried about my babies the whole time, locked up in that awful place."

Lucien said, "It's a perfectly adequate kennel."

His wife sent Dena a look that said, *What do men know?* "Now, I'm almost afraid to ask, Dena, but is there a Xanadu resort anywhere near Larchmont?"

"Well, our Litchfield location isn't too far from you."

Cynthia's face lit up. "Litchfield! No, that's not too far at all!" She turned to her husband once more. "We can leave our babies at Xanadu when we go to Tahoe next month."

"We'll discuss it," Lucien said.

His wife waved her hand dismissively. It was clear that as far as she was concerned, the decision was made.

"You might know some of our clients in your area," Dena said, knowing a little name-dropping would go a long way with Gabe's mother. "Elliot and Abigail Drinkwater have boarded their prize-winning Abyssinian cats with us three times already, and the Litchfield location has only been open since June."

Cynthia looked suitably impressed. Elliot Drinkwater was a well-known commercial real estate mogul. "Did you hear that, Lucien? We met the Drink-waters at Cloris's New Year's open house."

Dena said, "Lena Demopoulos—the movie producer?—left her Jack Russell terrier with us for three weeks when she went to Greece. When she arrived to pick him up, he didn't want to leave!"

"Gabriel, you've been very selfish," his mother scolded, "keeping our darling Dena all to yourself."

"Can't imagine what I was thinking," he said.

"I can't *wait* to tell Marjorie Wentworth about Xanadu," Cynthia said, with gleeful anticipation. "That woman thinks she's on the cutting edge of every new trend. I'll just *happen* to mention dropping Amber and Topaz off at the luxurious pet resort in Litchfield."

"Actually," Dena said, "you don't have to drop the dogs off unless you want to. We offer pickup service."

Gabe's father finally spoke up. "For which your customers pay dearly, I assume."

His wife raised an eyebrow. So low that Dena barely heard it, she muttered, "Shall we discuss how much that new sloop of yours set us back?"

"Don't be silly." Dena waved her hand negligently. "Naturally there'd be no charge for pickup and dropoff. Not for *you*," she added, in her chummiest tone.

Gabe's mother bestowed a smile of such warm affection, Dena could only wonder if she remembered she was talking to "the janitor's daughter."

As waiters arrived with the next course, Cynthia politely asked after Dena's parents—"Maine! How lovely! The Prescott Webleys retired to Maine just last year. I must ask them if their paths have crossed." She insisted Dena alert her the next time her folks visited, so they could meet for lunch. By the time the dinner plates were being cleared, history had been rewritten and Cynthia Moreau had always known that "our darling Dena" would make them all proud.

Gabe found Dena's hand under the table and squeezed it. He leaned toward her. "I don't know how you did that, love. I'm just glad you didn't decide to go into law. I'd hate to have to go up against you in a courtroom."

"You shouldn't be so surprised," she whispered. "Wasn't it you who told me I'd win them over?" She glanced at his father. "One down, one to go."

Gabe's sigh said he wasn't so optimistic.

Lucien abandoned his seat and came toward them, putting her instantly on the alert. "Would you care to join me on the dance floor, Dena?"

She made herself smile. "I'd love to."

The band began "Strangers in the Night" as the two singers, a man and a woman, lent their excellent voices to the sentimental lyrics. Gabe's father danced her away from the other couples on the floor. Dena tried to match his relaxed confidence, but apprehension made her stiff and graceless.

He remained silent, which only increased her anxiety. But of course, that was his intention, she realized. He was trying to rattle her.

"That was quite a performance you gave," he said at last. His pleasant expression never faltered, even when he added, "Gabe should have known better than to bring you here. He had more sense when he was a kid."

Dena knew he was referring to that disastrous

night fifteen years ago when Gabe had "sensibly" escorted Andrea to a function similar to this one. Obviously his father didn't know what had happened out there on one of the club's manicured fairways, and it wasn't Dena's place to enlighten him.

She asked, "Has it occurred to you that your son might actually love me?"

"I don't doubt he thinks so. I would have hoped that at his age he'd know better than to get carried away by a fling."

"A fling?"

"You're the forbidden fruit, Dena. Too exciting to resist. Just as you were back in high school." He shrugged. "A normal male response, I suppose. The problem is, Gabe can't seem to tell the difference between the kind of woman one shares one's life with and the kind of woman one shares one's bed with."

Reflexively Dena tried to pull away, but he tightened his grip on her fingers and her waist, still moving fluidly to the music. Dena glanced toward their table. She wasn't surprised to find Gabe's eyes on her, even as Andrea slid into Dena's vacated seat.

"No need to act offended," Lucien said. "I'm no puritan. What you and my son do in private is of no concern to me."

"As long as it stays private, is that right? As long as I'm kept hidden away. The dirty little secret. The trashy 'fling' who knows her place."

He chuckled. "You make it sound so sordid. Men and women have enjoyed each other's company throughout history. Not every relationship is meant to end in marriage."

"Oh, so I'm a mistress?" she asked. "How downright Victorian. I feel much better now. You know, you don't have to crush my fingers, Mr. Moreau. I'm not going to stalk off the dance floor or slap your face or do anything else that might embarrass Gabe. No matter how much I may be tempted."

Lucien's smile was unpleasant. "You'll pardon me if I have my doubts." If anything, he squeezed her fingers tighter.

Smiling sweetly, Dena pressed her stiletto heel into his instep. Hard. He sucked in a breath, his features rigid. After a moment he loosened his grip on her hand.

"Oops." Dena smiled apologetically as she lifted her heel. "I get clumsy when I'm riled up."

He stared sullenly at her. "There's a disagreeable edge to your personality that was never there before. I'm surprised Gabe puts up with it."

"It's called self-respect, and Gabe likes it just fine."

I NEVER SHOULD HAVE brought her here, Gabe thought as he watched his father lead Dena around the dance floor. Dad's impassive facade had slipped; he looked downright menacing. What was he saying to her?

Damn it, this hadn't been part of the plan. *Stick with me,* Gabe had told her. He'd intended to keep her at his side the whole evening, do all the talking, show her she had nothing to fear.

He was debating the wisdom of trying to cut in on the dance when Andrea's nasal voice intruded.

"You look worried," she said, following his line of sight to the dance floor.

When had she planted herself in Dena's chair?

Gabe looked around the empty table. "Where's Spencer?"

She nodded across the room. "Cozying up to Dad. Spencer was passed over for partner at Manning McLeod, and now he's got his sights set on us."

"It doesn't bother you that he's probably just using you as an entrée into the firm?"

Andrea's smirk was more than a little suggestive. "Ask me tomorrow morning."

Gabe didn't comment. Despite the image Andrea cultivated of a thick-skinned, independent, sexually liberated woman, he suspected that deep down, she was very lonely. He felt sorry for her, though he was careful not to show it.

"You didn't answer me," she said.

"You didn't ask a question."

"I'd be worried, too," she said as she watched Dena dance and converse with his father. "There's no telling what she'll come out with next. Whatever possessed you to bring her here, Gabe?"

He was asking himself the same question, but for different reasons. What had possessed him to subject the woman he loved to this kind of strain? She'd handled his mother with admirable ease, but Lucien Moreau was in a different league. Gabe had seen him verbally slice and dice the most stalwart of adversaries in the court of law.

Dena may not be the same "scaredy-cat" she'd been back in high school, but she didn't stand a chance against his shark of a father. She didn't deserve whatever abuse he was heaping on her right now, and she sure as hell didn't deserve to be treated like a pariah. She was worth this whole pretentious lot put together.

What if she succumbed to Dad's bullying—or simply decided Gabe wasn't worth a lifetime of this kind of aggravation? He had to admit, he wouldn't blame her if she walked out of his life. For good this time.

"One word of advice," Andrea said. "If you're determined to throw her in everyone's face, at least teach her how to dress."

DENA'S PATIENCE WAS STRETCHED to the limit. "What else did you want to say, Mr. Moreau? This song'll be over in a minute and I'm not sticking around for the next one."

Lucien glowered at her. His color was a little high under the suntan. "I'm prepared to pay you fifty thousand dollars."

She nearly tripped. "Excuse me?"

"Fifty thousand, Dena. Think what that kind of money could do for those kennels of yours."

"Mr. Moreau. Tell me you're not trying to *bribe* me to give up your son."

"It's an unsuitable match. He's obviously far too serious about you, and it's affecting his judgment."

"Gabe is thirty-three years old. Don't you think it's high time you stopped trying to run his life?"

"What I think is that it's high time he settled down. He needs a woman appropriate to his station in life, a woman reared with the same values, a woman who will be an asset to his career—not a liability and an embarrassment, which is what you'd become the first time he asked you to help entertain an important client."

Lucien should know that wasn't true, having witnessed her interchange with Helmut Danziger. But he obviously had his mind made up and didn't want to be confused with the facts.

"If you have any feelings for my son at all," he said, "you'll let him go."

"So he can marry Andrea Pittman."

"I haven't given up hope. It's an ideal match."

"You're delusional if you believe that, Mr. Moreau. Gabe and Andrea both know it's not meant to be."

"When Gabe was young he resisted the idea, simply because he knew it was what his mother and I wanted. Typical youthful rebellion. Now, however, he's more mature and realistic. He and Andrea both have a better understanding—"

"You're not listening," she said. "They're incompatible. They tolerate each other for the sake of the firm, but they'll never be close friends, much less life partners."

"Fifty thousand, Dena. It's a onetime offer."

"You're embarrassing yourself, Mr. Moreau. Bribing me is beneath you. Whatever our differences in the past, at least I never doubted your integrity."

Lucien flinched as if she'd stomped his foot again. He started to speak, and glanced around as if to ensure no one was within earshot. Without meeting her eyes he murmured, "You needn't call it a bribe. What I'm suggesting is a simple business arrangement."

"It's a bribe, Mr. Moreau. You know it. I know it. I wouldn't have taken your money when I was dirt-poor. I'm sure as hell not going to jump at it now, when Xanadu is worth over five million dollars."

His eyes flared. "I don't believe you."

"Ask Andrea. She made it her business to find out my net worth, right before she tried to raid me away from Gilliam, Shapiro."

Lucien's throat worked. He fixed his gaze on a point past Dena's shoulder. The song was winding down.

When he spoke, his voice was tight. "If I've been, perhaps…overzealous, it's because I have my son's best interests at heart."

"I know that," she said gently.

He studied her intently. "Do you love him?"

"Yes. I love him very much, and I'll do my best to make him happy."

Forever, Gabe had said. Suddenly Dena knew she'd settle for nothing less.

Lucien looked toward their table. Gabe was scowling at something Andrea had said. "You won't mention the…business arrangement we discussed?"

"He won't hear about it from me."

Dena suspected Lucien wanted to apologize but was too proud. Still, she didn't delude herself. She knew he'd be happy to see her exit his son's life for good. Perhaps he'd always feel that way. If so, she'd settle for a policy of noninterference.

A sardonic half smile creased Lucien's face. "Thank you for the dance, Dena." He started to lead her toward their table.

She smiled, too. "How's your foot?"

"Next time I get you riled up, I'll make sure you're wearing sneakers."

AFTER THAT CRACK about teaching Dena to dress, Gabe gave Andrea his undivided attention. He stared at her until she started to squirm.

"Tell me," he said. "Have your parents ever heard about that little escapade on the golf course?"

The lingering vestiges of her smirk faded away. Gabe knew the answer. The Pittmans didn't have a clue about that night, any more than his parents did. Bob and Gwen would have been horrified to learn that their precious teenage daughter had doggedly seduced their best friends' son when she was supposed to be making a favorable first impression on her future colleagues. Even now, they probably thought there were two or three discreet lovers in her past, tops.

And Andrea wanted to keep it that way.

"Are you threatening me?" That telltale flush crept up her throat.

"I've had enough of your meddling," Gabe said. "It stops as of now."

"Who the hell do you think you are?"

"No more of your snide comments to Dena," Gabe said. "All the little jabs and innuendoes. You know what I'm talking about."

"I never thought I'd see you lose your head like this over some—"

"Don't say it," he warned. "I mean it, Andrea. Personally, I don't give a damn what you think of Dena. You don't have to like her. You *do* have to treat her with the courtesy and respect she deserves."

Andrea glanced quickly around, and snapped, "You're as overbearing as your old man. What makes you think you can dictate to me?"

"I'm under no illusions that your malevolence is motivated by jealousy. It's wounded pride, pure and simple. You just can't stand it that Dena wouldn't let you add Xanadu to your client roster. You shouldn't have tried it, Andrea. We discussed it."

"You're bluffing." She stood and smoothed out her gown. "If you were going to blab about that night, you'd have done it long ago."

He smiled. "Maybe I never had a reason."

She shrugged. "And maybe I don't care who finds out about the golf course. That youthful folly happened a long time ago. If anything, it's an amusing anecdote. Who'd get excited about it at this late date?"

Gabe laughed. "I can only pray you never bluff that clumsily in the courtroom."

Andrea gave him what she no doubt considered a withering glare and hied herself off to the bar.

Gabe suddenly realized "Strangers in the Night" had ended. The band was now playing "Isn't It Romantic?" He leaped to his feet and scanned the dance floor. Dena and his father were no longer on it. Someone tapped his shoulder and he spun around to find Dena standing there with Dad.

Gabe was in no mood to mince words. He slid his arm protectively around Dena and looked his father in the eye. "Okay, what did you do to her?"

Dad looked affronted. "I didn't do anything to her!"

"You know what I mean." Gabe pulled the two of them a little farther from the nearest knot of people and growled, "I know you weren't making small talk about the weather. What did you say to her, Dad?"

"What this young lady and I discussed is between us."

"Don't give me that. I know how—"

"May I say something?" Dena asked.

"No. I know how you feel about her," Gabe told his father. "I wish it were different, and I hope someday you do feel differently, once you get to know her and find out what an incredible woman she is, but—"

"This is not necessary," Dad said.

"*But*," Gabe persisted, "ultimately it makes no difference to me how you feel about Dena. About us. Because I love her and I'm keeping her and you'll just have to get used to it."

His father waited patiently for him to continue.

Gabe was a little out of breath after his tirade. "That's all I have to say."

Lucien gave a small nod to acknowledge his son's position. Then he said simply, "I don't approve."

Gabe waited. "That's it?" he said at last. "You don't approve?"

Dena said, "May I say something?"

Distracted, Gabe waved her to silence. "Dad, I know you have more to say on the subject than that. Let's have it."

"Will it make a difference?"

"Hell no."

"Then what would be the point?"

Gabe turned his incredulous gaze on Dena. "What did you do to him?"

She rolled her eyes.

Dad examined one of his black patent-leather shoes. "Nothing that an ice bag and a dry martini won't cure."

"What *happened* out there?" Gabe demanded.

Dena appeared to give it some thought. "Let's just say your father and I have come to an understanding of sorts."

"An understanding," Gabe parroted.

Dad was looking at Dena with something akin to respect. Grudging respect, but respect nonetheless. "May I get you a drink, my dear?"

"I'd better go with you," she told his father. "Looks like you've got a bit of a limp there."

As Gabe watched them disappear through the crowd, he knew that fifty or sixty years with this remarkable woman wasn't going to be nearly enough.

"Isn't It Romantic?" was winding down. He made his way across the dance floor, stepped onto the band's stage and asked the lead singer for the microphone. He faced the packed ballroom.

"It has recently come to my attention," Gabe said into the mike, as conversation stilled and all eyes turned to him, "that certain partners and staff have been involved in illegal wagering on office property."

He heard a few snickers.

"The subject of this wagering is purported to be the matrimonial prospects of yours truly."

This was met with sprinkled applause.

Gabe placed a hand on his chest and affected an air of wounded dignity. "I'm told that people have been placing cash bets based on evidence that is circumstantial at best. Such evidence includes lapses in concentration, an uncharacteristic spring to my step, and what has been described as a—" he crooked his fingers to indicate quotation marks "—'sappy grin.'"

The crowd's enthusiastic agreement turned to groans when Gabe added, "Also, I understand I've been humming 'It Had to Be You.'

"As some of you have learned firsthand this evening, there is indeed a special lady in my life. Her name is Dena Devlin. Dena's a shy, unassuming little thing, but maybe, if we're very lucky, she'll come out here and say hi. Dena? How about it?"

After a moment the crowd parted and Dena sailed through in all her striking, statuesque glory, as shy and unassuming as a parade float. The organza petals of her skirt billowed behind her as she strode into the clearing in front of the stage on which Gabe stood, with the twenty-piece band arrayed behind him. As she made her grand entrance, one of the saxophones launched into the first few bars of "It Had to Be You."

A handful of guests did stare at Dena and murmur to one another, Gabe noticed, but most welcomed her with spirited applause. There were even one or two wolf whistles. For her part, she smiled and spread her arms in a well-here-I-am gesture, and the crowd went wild.

Gabe held up his hand for quiet. Into the mike he said, "Dena, these folks want to know if you and I are getting married."

There were several shouts of "Yeah!" and one Teutonic-sounding *"Ja!"*

Dena stepped onto the stage, with an assist from Gabe. She took the mike from his hand and they shared it. "I'd be happy to satisfy their curiosity, Gabe, but I don't recall having been asked."

Cries of "Ask her!" filled the ballroom.

Gabe looked into her gorgeous green eyes. "Dena, will you marry me?"

Gravely she shook her head. Gabe's heart sank like a lead weight until she said, "That's not how you ask."

The male guests instructed him with shouts of "Do it right!" and "Get down on your knee!"

Obediently Gabe went down on one knee. Behind him the band's drummer executed a drumroll. Dena held the microphone near his mouth.

He clutched his heart. "Is this better?"

"I'm waiting."

"I don't have a ring."

"Good. I'll pick out the biggest diamond I can find. Now, get on with it!"

"Dena, my love, will you do me the honor of marrying me?"

She answered with a jubilant, full-throated whoop that was probably heard in Boston, followed by, "*Yes! Yes! Yes!*"

Then she was in his arms and the crowd was surging around them and the band was playing the most exuberant, discordant version of the wedding march he'd ever heard.

Gabe held her tight and looked out over the ballroom. He spotted his parents. His mother was ecstatic, weeping happy tears, basking in the congratulations being bestowed on her. His father stood a little apart. He caught his son's eye and, after a moment, raised his martini glass in a silent toast.

It wasn't much, but for Lucien Moreau, it was

astounding. But then, Gabe doubted his old man had been prepared for the janitor's daughter all grown up.

The crowd took up the chant of "Kiss her!" and Gabe complied, treating Dena to a toe-curling clinch that had the younger, less staid segment of their audience hooting in encouragement. Even the stodgier guests couldn't keep from smiling.

Breathless, Dena looped her arms around his neck. "Remember when I said a kiss of yours is still just a kiss?"

"Yeah?"

"I lied."

I was right, Gabe thought as he kissed that sexy lopsided grin off her face. Fifty or sixty years was definitely not going to be enough.

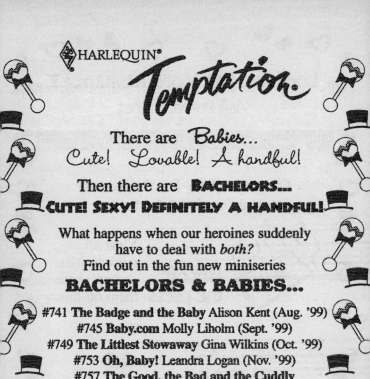

 HARLEQUIN®
Makes any time special ™

In celebration of Harlequin®'s golden anniversary

Enter to win a *dream!* You could win:

- A luxurious trip for two to *The Renaissance Cottonwoods Resort* in Scottsdale, Arizona, or
- A bouquet of flowers once a week for a year from FTD, or
- A $500 shopping spree, or
- A fabulous bath & body gift basket, including **K-tel**'s *Candlelight and Romance* 5-CD set.

Look for **WIN A DREAM** flash on specially marked Harlequin® titles by Penny Jordan, Dallas Schulze, Anne Stuart and Kristine Rolofson in October 1999*.

 FTD

 **RENAISSANCE. COTTONWOODS RESORT** SCOTTSDALE, ARIZONA **K·TEL**

*No purchase necessary—for contest details send a self-addressed envelope to Harlequin Makes Any Time Special Contest, P.O. Box 9069, Buffalo, NY, 14269-9069 (include contest name on self-addressed envelope). Contest ends December 31, 1999. Open to U.S. and Canadian residents who are 18 or over. Void where prohibited.

PHMATS-GR

"Don't miss this, it's a keeper!"
—**Muriel Jensen**

"Entertaining, exciting and
utterly enticing!"
—**Susan Mallery**

"Engaging, sexy...a fun-filled romp."
—**Vicki Lewis Thompson**

See what all your favorite authors
are talking about.

Coming October 1999 to a retail store near you.

 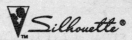

COMING NEXT MONTH

#749 THE LITTLEST STOWAWAY Gina Wilkins
Bachelors & Babies

Pilot Steve Lockhart thrived on challenges, and he was facing a big one. He'd just started up his own air charter service, when he'd gone and fallen in love with sexy Casey Jansen, the girl of his dreams—*and* the competition. He had to have her. And the newborn baby he discovered in his plane was going to help him....

#750 FOUR MEN & A LADY Alison Kent
15ᵗʰ Anniversary Celebration!

When gorgeous golden boy Ben Tannen offered Heidi-from-the-wrong-side-of-the-tracks Malone money for college tuition, she lashed out—with a bicycle chain! Now fifteen years later at their high school reunion, Ben wants an apology...and the chance to prove they'd make better lovers than fighters....

#751 ABOUT LAST NIGHT... Stephanie Bond
The Wrong Bed

When Janine Murphy sneaks into her fiancé's hotel room for a wedding night preview, she's in for a shock. The man she's sharing a bed with is strong, sexy, irresistible...but he's *not* her fiancé! Derek's the best man. And definitely the *better* man...for Janine.

#752 WANTON Lori Foster
Blaze

P.I. Alec Sharpe wanted to keep Celia Carter safe, while she wanted to be in on the investigation. Alec also wanted to make love to her, while Celia was determined to fight her wanton nature. The compromise? Alec would help her play P.I. if she would give in to their craving for each other...